THE WHITE PAVILION

Also by Velda Johnston

The White Pavilion

VELDA JOHNSTON

A Novel of Suspense

DODD, MEAD & COMPANY

NEW YORK

ISBN: 0-396-06851-0
Library of Congress Catalog Card Number: 73-7484
Printed in the United States of America
by Vail-Ballou Press, Inc., Binghamton, N.Y.

Johnston

For my niece Laurie Solum

One

Dolor Island is in the hands of an estate agent now. A recent letter from him says that a group of naturalists may buy it as a wildlife refuge. I'm glad. It would be good to think of excited school children, laden with binoculars, wandering the subtropical woodland—that same tangle of palmettos and live oaks and slash pines through which I followed a tall figure one night, not knowing that soon I would be face to face with my own death.

As for the house, perhaps it will become the administration building. Stenographers' heels will click cheerfully along those downstairs corridors that were always too dark because of shrubbery crowding close to the windows. And perhaps business machines will clatter in that upstairs room where my Aunt Evelyn lay, arrogant, unrepentant, and yet with a sense of some shadowy retribution closing in.

Of course, I can't be sure that the sale to the naturalists actually will be made. All I am sure of now is that

1

never again will I drive over the causeway, as I did that afternoon last August, then through the gate in the high steel fence guarding the island's landward side, and then up the tree-bordered road toward the house where my mother had been born and her sister still lived.

I had not wanted to come there. Oh, not because of any premonition. Perhaps unfortunately, I seldom have premonitions. It was just that I had stayed briefly in that house as a child, and so had little reason to like my Aunt Evelyn.

Her letter, though, had sounded not only urgent but, in the light of my childhood memories of her, downright cordial. "I have a broken leg," she had written. "A mare I had the the bad judgment to buy threw me. I've sold the beast since, you may be sure. But since it could have been my neck rather than my leg, I've begun to think of putting my affairs in order, as your grandfather would have phrased it. To that end, I want someone to make an inventory and evaluation of the contents of this house—furniture, silver, your grandfather's collections, and so on. I hesitate to trust an outsider to even handle some of these things, let alone give me an accurate appraisal. With the expertise you must have gained in such matters by now, you should be just the person for the job.

"Besides, Jennifer, it would be good to see you again after all these years. Sixteen of them! You were only six that summer. Or was it seven?

"Anyway, please come for as many weeks as you can spare me. I'll do my best to make you comfortable."

There was a postscript: "As you'll notice from the return address, my name is no longer Dunway, but Clayton. I was married last March."

The Saturday after Aunt Evelyn's letter arrived at my New York apartment, I took it with me up to Aurora, the shabby old Hudson River town where I grew up, and where my mother still lives. My mother, incidentally, is Madge Langley, a Big Band era vocalist of whom you may have heard. She is also a writer of whom you have never heard, because all her work appears anonymously in magazines devoted to Real Stories from Actual Life.

In her cheerfully cluttered living room, my mother read the letter and then said wonderingly, "So she married Ben Clayton. Do you remember him, Jenny? He was your Aunt Evelyn's lawyer."

I nodded. During that long-ago summer a Mr. Clayton, a handsome man with graying brown hair, had appeared at the Dunway house several mornings, briefcase in hand. Each time he had stayed for lunch. Afterward he and Aunt Evelyn had played chess in the dark-paneled library which adjoined the dining room. My impression was that my aunt had always won. At least each time that I had peeked cautiously through the library doorway, she had been sitting back, exhaling cigarette smoke through her classic nose, and smiling across the chessboard at Mr. Clayton's bent head.

"I don't suppose I should be surprised," my mother went on. "Her Christmas card—oh, I don't know how many years back—mentioned that Ben's wife had died. I guess it's just that Evelyn always seemed too—too superior to want to marry anyone except Ray."

Ray Langley was my father. You might just possibly have heard of him. He was the pianist with Bud Easterly's Orchestra.

"And I don't think she took even Ray seriously. It was just that she couldn't understand why—"

She broke off, but I knew what she meant. Why hadn't Ray tried to marry the undeniably beautiful Dunway sister? Why instead had he chosen the younger one, who at best must have been described by her contemporaries as "cute-looking"? Come to think of it, she is still cute-looking, with big brown eyes and a freckle-dotted nose which sometimes give her the aspect of a teen-ager—yes, even now, when there are lines at the corners of the brown eyes and her hair owes its honey shade, no longer to nature, but to regular applications of something called Always Blond.

"The children," my mother said. "I wonder where they are."

"What children?" I asked patiently. I am used to those conversational leaps of hers.

"Ben Clayton's. It seems to me he had some children, or at least one. Do you remember anything about that?"

"No." Perhaps because I was lonely and frightened during those two months on Dolor Island—months that were like years to a seven-year-old—my memories of that time are vivid. But even so, there are gaps in my recollection. I could recall no children accompanying Mr. Clayton, nor any talk of them.

"Mother, do you think I should go down there?"

"Why not, dear? The shop will stay closed until after Labor Day, won't it?"

I nodded. In sweltering July and August, Manhattan is deserted by the ladies with Vuiton handbags and the gentlemen with thirty-five-dollar haircuts. Lacking customers, such carriage-trade establishments as the Unicorn Antique Shop close their doors.

"Besides, Jenny, that house will be yours someday."

"Are you sure?" I asked dryly. "Aunt Evelyn has a husband now."

She looked momentarily bewildered, and then shocked. "Oh, no! She wouldn't leave her property to Ben. Evelyn and I never got on well, even before Ray came along, but she wouldn't leave everything to an outsider. After all, if my father hadn't gotten so angry over my running off with Ray—"

But he had been angry—angry enough to cut his younger daughter off without a cent.

My mother said wistfully, "That last heart attack of his. I always think that if it hadn't happened until after you were born, Dad might have forgiven me."

"Never mind. We've made out fine."

I felt we had. My mother's stories had paid off the mortgage on this house and part of my expenses at New York University. I had met the rest by working Saturdays and summer vacations at the Unicorn Shop. Since graduation I had been a full-time employee. Just before she closed the shop in July, Mrs. Grunwald, the owner, had hinted that she might make me a junior partner someday.

My mother said, "Jenny darling, don't you want to go to your Aunt Evelyn's?"

I hesitated. My mother must have known, if only from my hysterical joy in my reunions with her and my father, how much I had missed them that long-ago summer. But, childlike, I had never complained to them about my aunt's treatment of me. Perhaps I had been unable to phrase my grievances. Or perhaps I had felt that my aunt, being an adult, was right in whatever she chose to do. Anyway, I had kept silent. And over the

5

years I had come to feel that perhaps my child's eyes had not seen my aunt truly. Perhaps she, a woman inexperienced with children, had felt that the somewhat overindulged child left in her care would benefit by a few weeks of stern discipline.

"I know Evelyn's rather difficult," my mother went on. "And I know it will be terribly hot down there this time of year. But with all her money, surely she's had the house air-conditioned. And after all, your grandfather made those collections."

A yearning note in her voice told me how often these past sixteen years she had hoped to see her childhood home again. But the hinting letters she had written to her sister had never elicited an invitation, any more than her occasional requests for a small loan—"just until the magazine pays me"—had resulted in a check. Aunt Evelyn's brief replies had cited her own heavy expenses, chided my mother for her muddle-headedness about money—which is real enough, heaven knows—and suggested that she seek some more steady source of income than that provided by magazines which pay only upon publication.

"I'll go. I may as well start down there tomorrow." When I told her about it later, my mother might feel that she herself, vicariously, had returned to Dolor Island.

I glanced at my watch. "I'd better get back to New York and start packing."

As we moved toward the front door, I paused beside my mother's desk with its upright typewriter, chewed yellow pencils, and thin stack of yellow pages. The typescript on the top page had many x'd-over lines.

"How's the work coming?"

6

She moaned. "Beulah gave me a terrible coverline this time."

Beulah was the editor of several magazines for which my mother had written almost exclusively during the past two years. It was Beulah's custom to think up "coverlines"—titles of an eye-popping nature—which would appear on the magazines' covers. The writer's task was to concoct a story to fit the title.

"What is the coverline?"

My parent said dismally, " 'Forced to Watch My Own Funeral.' "

"Wow!" I put my arm around her shoulders. "Well, you'll come up with something. You always do."

In my little bug I drove back to New York. There I dispatched a telegram to Mrs. Benjamin Clayton, Dolor Island, Florida. After that I phoned to break a dinner date for the next night. Still later, I called a friend who shared a room with two other girls in a women's hotel, offered her the use of my apartment for a month, and hung up with her glad cries echoing in my ears. Then I moved about my studio—euphemism for no-bedroom—apartment, packing a bag with the most lightweight clothing I owned. As I did so, I recalled gratefully that my mother had made no objection when, a year ago, I had told her I wanted to live in New York. "I'll miss you," she said, "but after all, we'll see each other often. Just never open the door until you look through the peephole. And have yourself listed in the book as J. E. Langley, so you won't get obscene phone calls."

By nine the next morning I had left Manhattan, its towers looming ghostlike through smog, and was driving along the New Jersey Turnpike through a landscape that was like a foretaste of hell. Oil refineries belched black smoke. Occasionally an exhaust stack shot roaring flame, pale in the hazy sunlight. And stretches of marshland, which once must have been beautiful with waving grass and melodious with the cries of waterfowl, lay malodorous and silent, their scant vegetation a sickly yellow, and their meandering streams coated with iridescent oil. Like most VW's, mine does not boast air-conditioning. After I had rolled my windows up against the noxious smell, I soon began to swelter.

But across rural southern New Jersey and Delaware, I drove with the windows down. And once I was moving across the bridge that spans sparkling Chesapeake Bay, I began to lose the reluctant mood in which I had set out that morning. After all, I was no longer a helpless seven-year-old. If there had ever been a reason, outside of my childish imaginings, to fear Evelyn Dunway Clayton, that reason had vanished. And it was fun to drive down the nation's eastern border toward a destination that might prove almost unrecognizable to my adult eyes.

The adventurous turn of my spirits prompted me to leave the coastal highway for a longer but less crowded inland route. In the early afternoon, just after I crossed the Virginia border, I stopped for a hamburger beneath one of Mr. Johnson's hospitable orange roofs, and then drove on at a leisurely pace through North Carolina's fields of tobacco and soybeans. I had crossed the South Carolina line, and was driving through a cotton field with blossoms gilded by the late afternoon sun, when I realized that I had become tired. With thankfulness I saw a sign which indicated that a motel awaited me five miles farther on.

Somehow my bug developed a flat tire overnight. By the time I had eaten breakfast the next morning and had the tire changed in the motel garage, it was past eleven o'clock. Thus it was not until late afternoon that I angled eastward across Georgia's red clay pine barrens toward the coast and the Florida border.

Soon after I crossed the state line, I saw a gracious, white-pillared hotel with the words "Manor House" painted in shining gold leaf above its wide veranda. I smiled, thinking of how pleased Mother would be to hear that the hotel was not only still in business, but looking very spruce. It was to the Manor House that the Dunway sisters, out together on a rare double date, had gone with their escorts, one summer night more than twenty-five years in the past, to dance to Bud Easterly's Orchestra. And it was there, during the interval, that the red-haired young pianist had crossed to their table, introduced himself as Ray Langley, and lingered until he had been invited over to the island for a swim the next day. According to my mother, it was the elder sister who had invited him, not the one who, six weeks later, had run away to New York to meet and marry him.

Probably, I reflected, my mother had felt sorrowful that she'd had to leave home without her father's blessing or her sister's good will. But even so, the first carefree years of her marriage must have been happy ones, and not just because she and my father were in love. Under his tutelage her clear soprano voice, until then suitable only for church choirs, had developed the crisp, swinging style of the nineteen-forties. Bud Easterly had hired her, and she and my father had traveled coast-to-coast with the band. Listening to her old records, I have often imagined a ballroom of that period, with my red-haired father at the piano, and my blond mother at the microphone singing "The Last Time I Saw Paris" to a group of dancers who did not dance, but just stood below the bandstand swaying gently until Madge Langley finished her number.

By the time I was born, the Big Band era was drawing to a close, done in by rising costs and by a switch in public taste to small groups like the Modern Jazz Quartet. My mother stayed home with me, while my father took whatever jobs he could get—a night club date here, a college prom there, and, when he was lucky, a fairly long stretch with some TV studio orchestra. Only once again did my father and mother work together. Leaving me on Dolor Island where, surprisingly, Aunt Evelyn had said I might stay, they had accompanied Bud Easterly's reconstituted band on its disastrous attempt at a comeback tour, across a nation enthralled with rock music and its gyrating young high priest, Elvis Presley. In Denver, Bud Easterly, flat broke, had disbanded his organization. Even though I was almost demented with joy when my parents came for me, I sensed that all was not well with them. They were both thinner than before, and my father's eyes had an almost frightened look. Although of course I did not realize it then, it was the look of a man with only a few hundred dollars in the bank and a wife and child to feed.

On a foggy night a few weeks later, as he was crossing Forty-seventh Street to audition for a job with a TV orchestra, a speeding car struck him down. He died in the ambulance on the way to the hospital. The driver who killed him was never found.

Well, I thought, as I turned into a gas station, probably Ray and Madge Langley had known more happiness in their years together than many couples who live to celebrate their golden wedding.

I should turn left at the next crossing, the attendant told me in a thin Florida drawl. "That'll bring you to Galton Beach, little bitty old place. Causeway to Dolor Island's on the far side of town."

Galton Beach was indeed a little bitty old place, not the sizable town I remembered, and a sad-looking little old place, too. Scabrous stucco buildings, some false-fronted, flanked its potholed main street. Overalled men lounged on the sagging porch of the Galton Beach Hotel, the one movie house looked as if it had been closed for years, and the plate-glass window of Barney's Quick Lunch was so grimy that one might think that generations of outraged patrons had flung their hominy grits against it. But the coral causeway just south of the town, stretching over water gilded with sunset light, looked the same. I even remembered the wooden sign which stood planted on a steel pole near the entrance: "Private Causeway. Trespassers Will Be Prosecuted." The sign had been freshly repainted.

A breeze had sprung up, crinkling the shallow water and blowing through the VW's windows. Perhaps that was why, as I drove across the causeway, I felt suddenly chilled. Or perhaps it was the sight of the house roof, rising above the pines and live oaks on the island ahead. To divert myself from that faint unease, I thought, "New York girl returns to ancient ancestral home."

But it really wasn't that. My grandfather had been born, not on Dolor Island, but in a Georgia sharecropper's cabin. Able and ambitious, he had worked his way

11

through college, gone to New York, and, in the prosperous days after the First World War, made a killing in the stock market. Later he had bought a small island, complete with a 1790's house, off the northern Florida coast. He had married the daughter of a St. Petersburg doctor, fathered two daughters, and, after his wife died, sent them to an expensive private school near St. Augustine. But even with his fine house built by someone else's ancestors, he must never have forgotten the dilapidated shacks, infertile fields, and rough-mannered kinfolk of his boyhood. Perhaps that was why his younger daughter's marriage had filled him with unforgiving rage. Perhaps he felt that she, in marrying an obscure jazz musician, had slipped back toward the origins he had struggled so hard to escape.

I had almost reached the island now. Up ahead I could see the closed gate in the steel mesh fence that ran along the island's landward-side beach. It seemed to me that sixteen years ago the fence had been of barbed wire. But the green frame caretaker's cottage, in a small grove beyond the fence, looked much the same.

Memories were flooding back now. The caretaker had been a slender, olive-skinned young Jamaican. Once when I had wandered down to the gate, he had brought an empty oil drum out onto the cottage's tiny porch. Smiling gently, and beating out an accompaniment on the drum with the heels of his hands, he had sung to me a sad but beautiful song about a girl left "in Kingston town." What had been the caretaker's name? Charles? Henry? Whatever his name had been, it certainly was not he up there on the cottage roof now, hammering a shingle into place.

I tapped the horn. The man on the roof, shirtless

and in faded blue jeans, looked at me and then got to his feet. Thrusting the hammer into a back pocket, he moved with deliberate, sidewise steps down the sloping roof to the ladder and descended it. Then he walked toward the gate, a blond man in his late twenties, skin bronzed by the subtropical sun. He opened the gate narrowly to walk through it. Standing beside the VW, he said, "Yes?"

Some psychologists—almost invariably male, I've noticed—state that, sexually speaking, the female is not eye-oriented. A handsome male face or well-knit male body awakens in her at most an esthetic response. I have news for those gentlemen. They're wrong. At sight of those intensely blue eyes set in a blunt-featured face, and that bronze torso tapering from wide shoulders to a flat waist, I felt more than admiration. I had a sensation akin to, but more pleasant than, the one I have felt in swiftly descending elevators.

I said, "I'm Jennifer Langley, Mrs. Clayton's niece."

He nodded. No warmth came into his eyes.

Now it is true that I have never been one of Bert Parks's young ladies, parading in high heels, old-fashioned one-piece bathing suit, and Linda Darnell hairdo on that stage in Atlantic City. But I have had my share of dates, and even a few marriage proposals. Certainly I was not used to seeing that remoteness in a man's eyes.

I said, "Mrs. Clayton is expecting me."

"I know."

He moved back to the gate and opened it wide. I stopped my car halfway through. "Are you the caretaker here?"

Something flickered in his eyes. "More or less."

Now just what, I wanted to ask, does that mean? I

said, "What is your name?"

"Harley."

My irritation grew. I had not introduced myself as Miss Langley. I had given him my first name as well as my last. Couldn't he have paid me the same courtesy? I had an impulse to say, in young-lady-of-the-manor tones, "Very well, Harley. You may return to your duties." But something in the cool eyes under the brown-blond brows stopped me.

I transferred my foot from the brake to the gas pedal, nodded, and then drove up the narrow dirt road between the tangled walls of pines, palmettos, and giant ilex.

Two

The house lay ahead, invisible beyond a curve in the road. But at the moment, because of my annoyance with whatever-his-name-was Harley, I'd forgotten the house.

A girl on a bicycle came around the curve. At sight of me she rode to the shoulder of the road and stopped, one sneaker-clad foot planted on the ground. As I drew closer, I saw that she was tall, almost six feet, and wore faded chinos and a sleeveless white T-shirt, obviously with no bra under it. I also saw that she was eighteen or nineteen, and beautiful. Shoulder-length straight hair, lemon-colored, framed a tanned, flawless face set with gray eyes that were almost too wide apart.

Of the many changes I might have expected to find on the island, an invasion of huge and handsome blonds of both sexes was last on the list. Who was she? One of Aunt Evelyn's maids? Probably not, not with those looks.

Already chilled by my encounter with the man at the

gate, I did not stop, but merely slowed down and nodded. She returned the nod, full lips unsmiling, gray
eyes not just indifferent, but sullenly hostile.

"A hearty welcome, Jennifer," I thought, and drove
on around the curve.

There was the red-brick Georgian house, standing in
its grass-carpeted clearing. As I turned onto the circular
drive that led to its broad front steps, I saw that the
house was not only smaller than in my childhood memories, but far more beautiful. In the years between I
had learned to appreciate such architectural details as
those perfectly proportioned stone columns and that
graceful fanlight above the broad front door.

Should I drive around to the rear, where, if I remembered correctly, there was a large carriage house remod-
eled into a garage? No, the garage might be full, and
besides, my driving back there might be considered
presumptuous. I stopped, got out, and took my suitcase
from the bug's trunk. Then I paused at the foot of the
steps, half expecting Mrs. Shaughnessy, Aunt Evelyn's
housekeeper, to open the door and move toward me
with a welcoming smile. But I knew that was unlikely
to happen. In her Christmas card of some years back,
Aunt Evelyn had referred to "my new housekeeper, a
Cuban refugeee." She had not said what had become of
Mrs. Shaughnessy.

A harsh twittering above. I looked up at small black
forms shifting restlessly under the eaves. Now, at sunset, the starlings had come home to roost. The sound
they made was a familiar one, because my room's window, sixteen years ago, had been under the spot where
the birds clustered most thickly.

With an old sense of oppression creeping over me, I

looked at that window and remembered my bedtimes in this house. Mrs. Shaughnessy, a thin woman with a kindly face, coming in to help me undress and to turn down my bed. A rattle of rings as she drew curtains against the last of the daylight. Then she would leave the room.

I would lie there in the night lamp's feeble glow, stiff with apprehension. After a few minutes the door would open and my aunt would say, "All right, Jennifer. I will come back in ten minutes. If you are not asleep—"

She never finished the threat, nor did I ever ask her what it was. It was sufficient to know that she was sole ruler of my universe, now that my parents had vanished from it, and that she could do whatever she chose.

She would close the door. I would lie there, knowing that I would still be awake when she opened the door that second time, and desperately afraid she would know it. When the door opened again, I would lie rigid, eyes tightly closed, and trying not to breathe. Only once did I dare to open my eyes the merest slit and look at her standing there in the doorway. She was smiling. After perhaps a minute the door would close, and sometime after that I would drift off to sleep.

Now, remembering that smile, I could no longer tell myself that my aunt had been just a childless woman who had tried, however ineptly, to do her best for the small girl left in her charge. She had enjoyed the sight of me, desperately feigning sleep. In fact, she must have found it great fun to have Ray and Madge's child in her charge, if only for a few weeks.

Standing in the sunset light, I wished heartily that I had not come here. But I had. And one thing was certain. Aunt Evelyn would not stand in my bedroom doorway now. Swiftly, lest I give way to the childish impulse to get back into the VW and drive off, I climbed toward the porch.

Before I reached it, the door opened, and a plump woman in a pink nylon uniform came out. "Miss Langley?" Her accent, like her olive-skinned face, told me that she must be the Cuban refugee my aunt had mentioned.

"Yes, I'm Jennifer Langley."

"I am the housekeeper, Mrs. Escobar."

"How do you do? I've left my keys in the car. But if you like, I can drive it—"

"No. Someone will take care of it."

As she reached for my suitcase, I said, "Oh, please don't. I can manage."

"As you wish. Mrs. Clayton is napping now. She asked me to show you to your room."

I followed her across the entrance hall, its parquet floor gleaming dully in the faint light that filtered through the shrubbery screening the downstairs windows, and then up the spiral staircase. As I climbed, I remembered how, after my solitary lunch in my room —all my meals were served in my room—I sometimes sneaked down to sit on the stairs where the staircase curved. I don't know why I did it. Perhaps even the sound of Aunt Evelyn's voice, speaking to the waitress in the dining room, or to Ben Clayton as they sat over the chessboard in the library, was preferable to the silence of my room. Or perhaps I hoped to hear the crunch of tires over gravel, and then my mother's voice.

To my relief, Mrs. Escobar turned right at the top of the stairs. So I had not been assigned to my old room. Perhaps, I reflected, my aunt hoped that I had forgotten her nightly visits. In that case, she would not want to put me in that room where the starlings murmured outside the window, lest I be reminded.

At the end of the hall Mrs. Escobar led me past a table which held a telephone, and then into a pleasant corner bedroom. Its southern windows overlooked the circular drive. Through its eastern ones I could see the trees bordering the side lawn, their tops gilded with sunset light. Enough of that light lingered in the room to show me the walnut spool bed—American, circa 1830, I thought automatically—and the matching bureau and dressing table. Through an open door I could see a small bathroom walled with green tile.

Mrs. Escobar switched on a crystal-based lamp which stood on the dressing table. "Dinner will be at eight," she said. "Afterward Mrs. Clayton would like you to come to her room. It is on your right, at the other end of the hall."

"I remember. Won't my aunt be at dinner?"

"Oh, no. Mrs. Clayton has a broken leg."

"So she wrote me. But I thought that by now she might be on crutches."

"No, her leg is still in traction."

"Will Mr. Clayton be at dinner?"

After a moment Mrs. Escobar said, "I don't imagine so."

A closed expression had come over her face. Did she, I wondered, disapprove of Ben Clayton? Perhaps, although I remembered him as a pleasant man who had given me a tentative but warm smile the few times I had been in his presence.

"I'll send Lorena to help you unpack."

Lorena? The girl on the bicycle? If so, Lorelei would

19

have been a more appropriate name.

"Good-by," Mrs. Escobar said, and left me.

I had placed my suitcase on the bed coverlet of glazed chintz and opened its lid when a voice said, "Miss Langley, I presume?" And then, after I had turned around: "My, my! What the years have wrought."

He stood there in the doorway, a thin young man, dressed in dark trousers and a blue knitted sport shirt, with his curly dark hair falling over his forehead. Where before had I seen those hazel eyes and that forehead that wrinkled whenever he grinned that broad, teasing grin?

I said, "Kevin Shaughnessy!"

Kevin, son of that kindly woman who had been Aunt Evelyn's housekeeper. Kevin, that lordly boy, almost an adult in my seven-year-old eyes, who had sometimes condescended to let me tag along after him through the woods and down to the beach on the island's seaward side.

"You're pretty good," he said. "How old were you then?"

"Seven."

"And I was twelve. I'm twenty-eight now. Good Lord, sixteen years. May I comment that you turned out very well?"

"You may." Especially after my encounter with that cold-eyed blond giant at the gate, it was pleasant to see admiration in a man's eyes.

"Okay if I come in?"

"Of course." I sat down beside my suitcase. "Come in and have a seat."

He moved toward a chintz-covered armchair. With

shock I saw that he, who as a boy had swarmed up trees with the agility of a monkey and raced like a whippet along the beach, now walked with a limp.

Shock must have lingered in my face, because after he sat down, he said, "Pay that no mind. It's just a souvenir from Charlie."

It took me a moment or two to realize his meaning. "You were in Vietnam?"

He nodded. "Got back two years ago."

"How's your mother?"

After a moment he said, "She died five years ago, while I was still in 'Nam."

"Oh, Kevin! I had no idea. All Aunt Evelyn said was that she had a new housekeeper. And that was on a Christmas card. She seldom writes a letter to us."

"That I can believe."

I hesitated, and then asked, "What are you doing now?"

"I work here."

"Here!"

"Sure. In 'Nam I learned a lot about accounting. I was a supply sergeant there. And I still like to fool with machinery. Maybe you don't remember that about me."

"I remember."

"Well, there's a lot of machinery on this island. As you probably know, it has its own power plant, and a well with an electric pump."

I nodded, recalling how I had once stood near a circular cement building about a hundred yards behind the house, puzzled by the humming noise that issued from it, until Kevin had come up beside me and said, "That's the powerhouse, you little dope."

"So anyway," Kevin said, "after I was discharged, I

wrote to your aunt from New York, asking if she would like to have an accountant-and-engineer-in-residence, so to speak, instead of sending over to the mainland every time something went wrong. She wired me to come down, and when I did, she decided to hire me, even though I could tell this gimpy leg of mine didn't set well with her."

"Set well! You mean she *objected* to your limp?"

"I guess you were too young to realize it when you were here, but your aunt has always liked the men around her to be handsome, and sound of wind and limb."

Perhaps that was true. Even though Ben Clayton had seemed middle-aged to my child's eyes, he had been undeniably handsome, and no doubt still was. And certainly that Jamaican caretaker, like the one at present employed by her, had been good to look at.

"And so," Kevin went on, "I keep everything around here going pocketa-pocketa-queep, and I do the accounts, although you can bet she goes over my figures with a gimlet eye."

"I see." But I didn't, not really. Why should he, who evidently had grown into a man of ability, be content with such undemanding work? And why above all had he chosen to work for my aunt? Although I could not pin down the exact memory, I had the feeling that something had happened between my aunt and twelve-year-old Kevin that summer—something that would give him little reason to like her.

He grinned and then said, "What is it? You hung up on the old work ethic? I like my job, and I like this island. The swimming's good, and whenever I like I can drive over to St. Augustine and raise a little hell.

"Besides," he went on, "it's the only home I can remember. I was three years old when my mother came to work here."

I hadn't known that. With a stab of sympathy I thought of what it would be like to have no memory of your mother working in her own kitchen and presiding at her own table.

As if shying away from the subject, he said, "I guess your aunt's marriage was pretty much of a shock to you."

Puzzled, I answered, "Why should it? It's her business."

After a moment he said, "Well, it's good to know· you're broad-minded."

Why broad-minded? I was about to ask him when he looked at the doorway and said, "Hi, Lorena."

I turned my head, half expecting to see the blond Venus of the bicycle. Instead I saw a plump, swarthy-skinned girl wearing a uniform of unbecoming blue. She smiled at me. " 'Allo, mees." She added apologetically, "Not mooch Anglish."

"Come in, Lorena," I said.

She crossed to the bed and began to lift garments from the suitcase. Kevin stood up. "Guess it's time for me to leave. Oh, before I forget. Here are your keys. I put your car in the garage." He laid the keys on the dressing table. "Well, see you at dinner."

"You'll be there?"

"Sure. I have dinner table status around here."

"I'm glad." I paused. "Who else will be at dinner?"

"Your aunt's doctor is staying, I guess. At least I saw

him mixing himself a drink at the bar in the dining room a few minutes ago. And of course there'll be Amy."

"Amy?"

"Amy Warren. Sort of a permanent house guest here. She's psychic. Or maybe the word is psycho."

I glanced warningly at Lorena, who was laying folded garments in a bureau drawer. "Not much English," Kevin reminded me. He limped toward the door. "See you," he said, and left.

Lorena and I spent the next ten minutes settling my belongings in the closet and in the bureau. When she had gone, I took a quick shower and put on a sleeveless dress of green linen. I was running a comb through my hair when I heard a remembered sound—the dinner gong in the entrance hall below, reverberating softly through the house.

Three

"Are you interested in the Other World, Miss Langley?"

Laying down the heavy sterling fork with which I had been cutting Mrs. Escobar's excellent pompano, I looked across the dining table at the woman Kevin had introduced as Mrs. Warren. Beyond her shoulder I could see the doorway to the darkened library, that room which housed my grandfather's various collections, and which had been off limits to me as a child.

Uncomfortably I was aware that not only Amy Warren awaited my answer. Kevin, seated on the left side of the oval Sheraton table with a faint smile curving his mouth, obviously wondered what I would say. And of course Dr. Satherly, seated opposite him, must be listening, even though he kept his eyes fixed on his plate.

I said cautiously, "Do you mean heaven?"

She waved a heavily veined hand dismissingly. "Of course not. Heaven is a Christian superstition. I am a follower of the Old Religion."

I was disconcerted less by her words than by their contrast with her appearance. She was the sort of middle-aged woman you see over and over again all over America, emerging from under movie marquees in the late afternoon, or standing indecisively at the supermarket meat counter with a package of chopped steak in each hand, or smiling out from some small-town newspaper photograph of the Women's Civic Betterment Committee. Thin legs supporting a thickened but well-corseted body, tonight clad in a pink-and-yellow flowered print of some synthetic material. Permanently waved graying brown hair. Small gray eyes set behind butterfly glasses, their amber rims ornamented with rhinestones. A straight nose that hinted at brief prettiness in youth, a prim-looking mouth, and a sagging chin line.

I said feebly, "Then I'm afraid I don't—"

"I refer to the Other Plane, the world that is all around us, and yet invisible. Invisible to most of us, that is."

"But not to you, Mrs. Warren." Kevin was openly grinning now. He turned to me. "Mrs. Warren is a witch. She can explain the whole bag to you, clairvoyance, crystal gazing, even devil worship."

She looked at him coldly. "I do not worship the devil. I am a white witch. I use my powers for good. However," she went on, and now there was fury in the little eyes behind the rhinestone-rimmed glasses, "I acknowledge the devil's reality. And I think that you, of all people, must be aware of it, too."

Kevin's grin didn't waver, but I could sense his answering antagonism. For a moment, hostitity was an almost palpable force in the room. Embarrassed, I tried

26

to divert their attention to myself. I said, "I guess I'm just not psychic."

The look she gave me held faint commiseration. "No, your vibrations are not those of a sensitive. But if you are in the least open to psychic influences, you should be aware of them on this island. You know how it got its name, don't you?"

"Dolor Island? I always assumed it was named after someone. Not the people whose ancestors built this house. Their name was Haywood. But I thought that someone else, farther back—"

"I think that the island's name is Spanish. *Dolor* means pain, sorrow. A suitable name, considering that slaves used to be hidden here in the eighteen-thirties and forties."

"Slaves? But why hidden? Slavery was legal then."

"But the importation of slaves no longer was. Slavers would land them here at night, keep them hidden for a while, and then smuggle them over to the mainland, one by one or in small groups. But surely you knew that."

I shook my head. If my mother had known, she had never told me. And I wished this woman had not told me now. Where had those terrified men, women, and children been hidden? In the attic or cellar of this fine old house? Or had they been chained to trees somewhere out in that tangle of scrub pine, palmettos, and vine-enlaced hardwoods?

"No one knows whether or not any of the slaves actually died on this island," Amy Warren said. "But even so, I am sure the emotions they felt here must linger on in the atmosphere."

Could she possibly be right about that? If so, perhaps

27

I was a "sensitive" after all. Perhaps it was not just longing for my parents, or fear of Aunt Evelyn, which had oppressed my young spirit that summer. Perhaps I had sensed the anguish of some other child to whom, almost a century and a half ago, this island had been a far more terrible prison than it was to me.

I gave myself a mental shake. How silly to let this woman's vaporings get to me. I picked up my fork.

A Haywood fork, expensively heavy in the hand. Perhaps because he was in too much of a hurry to select his own things, or perhaps because he did not trust his own taste, my sharecropper-born grandfather had bought not only the island and the house, but its furniture, crystal, china, and silverware, too.

And if Amy Warren was right, the Haywoods had been slaverunners, pursuing their abominable trade for years after Congress had outlawed it. The pain and terror of helpless people had bought this handsome table, this fork in my hand . . .

I laid down my fork and turned to the man at my right. He was a thin man of late middle age, with light blue eyes behind rimless glasses, and a compressed mouth. From the moment Kevin had introduced us, I had felt that Dr. Satherly's personality was the tense, repressed sort described most aptly as "up tight."

I asked, "Are you interested in the occult?"

He gave a bleak little smile. "Hardly. I don't have time for the metaphysical. Dealing with the physical— my patients' problems, I mean—is hard enough."

I asked lightly, "Is my aunt a difficult patient?"

After a moment he answered, "Any active person who breaks a leg becomes a difficult patient."

"But it is more than that with Evelyn," Amy Warren

28

said. "Naturally, I can't speak of matters she has told me in confidence, but let me assure you, Doctor, she is under great strain."

Kevin said, "I've noticed that. She's been under a strain ever since you moved in here six months ago."

She turned to him, bright spots of color on her cheekbones. "Just what do you mean by that?"

"I mean that if she takes your spooky patter seriously—"

"Spooky patter! There is a lot I could tell you if I chose to, young man. But let's take one thing that you know about. Was it my spooky patter that killed the dogs? Was it?"

Kevin said calmly, "No, it was poison."

She leaned toward him. "But who poisoned them? Tell me that!"

Kevin shrugged. "Probably no one, intentionally. With all the pesticides around these days, you often find dead or dying animals in the woods, and dead fish on the beach. The vet said the Dobermans probably got hold of some animal that was loaded with an arsenic pesticide."

"The vet was only speculating." She looked across the table at me. "And your aunt was worried about trespassers long before I came here. That was why she bought the Dobermans."

I said, "Have there been many trespassers?"

Before Mrs. Warren could answer, the girl Lorena came into the room, wheeling a service cart. A concentrated look on her face, she removed the dinner plates slowly and carefully, as if she found the task a test of all her powers. When the maid had left the room, Amy Warren said, "Your aunt doesn't know how many trespassers there have been, but certainly there have been some."

Kevin said, "So she brought the Dobermans here in case the trespassers were real live people, and Mrs. Warren in case they weren't."

She gave him a withering look, and then turned back to me. "You had better let your aunt tell you about it. I see there is no point in trying to discuss it here."

An awkward silence settled down. I felt annoyed with Kevin. True, Amy Warren was irritating, like most people hipped on one subject. But probably she meant well. And she was many years Kevin's senior. After Lorena, still with that air of concentration, had served us lemon sherbet and then left the room, I smiled at Amy Warren. "How did you and my aunt meet?"

"In a beauty parlor, of all places. She was under the dryer next to mine, and she saw that I was reading a magazine that deals with the occult, and—well, she asked me here to lunch several times, and finally she suggested I stay with her for a while."

"You're not a native Floridian, are you?"

"Oh, no. I didn't come down to St. Augustine until after my husband's death ten years ago. Until then we both lived in a small Nebraska town. My husband kept books in the department store there."

Talk of the severity of northern winters carried us safely through dessert. Then Lorena returned, carrying a tray laden with a sterling coffee service and small china cups. "Place it here, Lorena," Mrs. Warren said. She smiled at me. "Since Evelyn's accident, I've been pouring the coffee. You don't mind, do you?"

30

"Of course not."

Dr. Satherly pushed back his chair. "If you'll excuse me, I won't have coffee. Mrs. Clayton wants me to look in on her again before I leave."

A few minutes later the rest of us left the table. Mrs. Warren went into the library—there was something in William James she wanted to look up, she said—and Kevin and I walked out into the hall. At the foot of the stairs I said, "Kevin, weren't you rather hard on Mrs. Warren?"

He looked a bit shamefaced. "Maybe. But she really hassles me. She's not only nuts. She's a Puritan and a snoop. Somehow she manages to find out things."

"What things?"

"That I smoke a little grass once in a while. And that when I go to St. Augustine it isn't for the sightseeing. She can't make any trouble for me—your aunt doesn't give a damn what I do, as long as I do my job—but I hate being spied on."

"Yes, I can see how you would." I started up the stairs and then turned back. "I've been meaning to ask you. When I drove in this afternoon, I saw a girl. She's tall and blond and very good-looking, and she was riding a bicycle toward the gate."

"That's Lisa Clayton. She lives here. I guess she was going over to Galton Beach."

"Clayton? Ben Clayton's daughter?"

"That's right."

"So," I said, "Aunt Evelyn has a stepdaughter as well as a husband."

An odd expression flitted across Kevin's upturned face. Then he laughed.

"What's so funny?"

"A joke. You'll get it before long. If I told you now, it would spoil it. Well, I've got to fix the damn riding mower yet tonight. See you around," he said, and moved toward the rear of the hall.

Four

I stayed in my room until I heard a car, presumably Dr. Satherly's, move away down the drive. Then I walked down the wide corridor, its polished floor shining in the light of crystal-shaded wall lamps, and tapped on Aunt Evelyn's door.

"Come in."

Sixteen years ago this big corner room had held a four-poster bed with a needlepoint canopy, a bed so magnificent that even though I could not have seen it more than once or twice, it remained clear in my memory. It was gone now, and in its place was a hospital bed of white metal. On it lay my aunt, a tall woman in a kaftan of peacock blue silk, her right leg held stiff by a pulley from the traction bar at the foot of the bed. She smiled at me and said, "Hello, Jennifer. Sit here so I can get a good look at you."

Aware of the contrast between that ugly bed and the softly gleaming eighteenth-century furniture in the room, I crossed to a straight chair beside her and sat down. Perhaps to my seven-year-old eyes she had appeared older than her years. Or perhaps she really had changed very little. Anyway now, at the age of forty-eight—or was it forty-nine?—she looked much as I remembered her. Dark hair brushed loosely back from her face. Dark, rather prominent eyes, a classic nose, and a full mouth that somehow managed to appear both sensual and hard.

With that cool amusement I remembered, her eyes were scanning my face. "You look much more like me than like Madge."

I made a polite murmur. But I really did not think that was the case. It is true that my hair, a medium brown in my early childhood, is now almost as dark as my aunt's. But I have my father's blue eyes and my mother's small-boned, five-foot-five figure.

"How is Madge? Still writing for those magazines?"
"Yes."

"How did she ever get started doing that, anyway?"

"It happened about a year after my father died. She saw this magazine cover advertising a story contest. She won third prize."

I remembered the mounting excitement in our little house during those evenings when, after her day selling dresses at the Milady Shop, she wrote that first story. And I remember the awe with which we had looked at that five-hundred-dollar check.

"And so that was the start of her illustrious career."

I said evenly, "Mother has done very well."

I think that the reason for her success with those highly emotional stories is that she feels them so deeply. Whenever I came home from school to find my mother at the typewriter, tears rolling down her cheeks, I never asked what disaster had struck us. I knew that she wept for one of her own creations—some young mother sitting helpless beside the bed of her stricken child, some aged couple denied shelter in the homes of their prosperous offspring.

My aunt shook a cigarette from the pack lying on her bedside table—a mahogany Queen Anne, I noticed—and lit it with a thin gold lighter. I took the opportunity to throw a sweeping look around the room. A Directoire chaise lounge upholstered in dark red satin, over there by the long windows which led onto the rear balcony. Perfume bottles and a silver-backed comb and long-handled silver brush on a Queen Anne dressing table. No military brushes. No sign of masculine occupancy anywhere. I looked at the partially opened door leading to a bathroom with a marble, gold-spigoted washbasin. Her husband's room, probably, was the connecting one beyond the bath.

My aunt said belatedly, "Have a cigarette?"

"Thank you, but I don't smoke."

"Smart girl. I'm grateful to you for coming down here. Now do you remember your grandfather's collections at all?"

I wanted to say, "The library was off limits to me, remember?" Instead I said, "No, I don't."

"Well, mainly he collected miniatures, snuffboxes, rare coins, and seashells."

"I'm afraid I don't know anything about coins or shells."

"That's all right. Harley can help you with the shells. I've gathered that he knows quite a lot about them. And as for the coins, I ordered a coin catalogue for you three weeks ago, right after I broke my leg."

Three weeks ago, before she had written to me. Evidently she had been confident I would come here.

"And then there's the furniture and crystal and china, plus a lot of bric-a-brac that may be valuable or practically worthless."

"I shouldn't have any trouble with all that."

"Fine. Now how is your room? Did Mrs. Escobar and her niece make you comfortable?"

"Yes, thank you. But I didn't know Lorena was the housekeeper's niece." I paused. "Isn't Lorena a bit—"

"Stupid? Very. She's been in this country for two years, and worked for me for almost a year, and she still hasn't learned more than a few words of English."

She ground out her cigarette in a crystal ashtray. "But that is what makes her such a jewel. Stupid maids are the best for simple household tasks. The work demands all their attention, and so they don't get bored."

She added, "Did you enjoy your dinner?"

"It was delicious."

"And Amy Warren? What did you think of her?" Her eyes, narrowed now, scanned my face.

"She seems—quite sincere."

"I find her a barrel of laughs. She's been here six months." A wave of her long hand indicated the bathroom door. "Amy has the next room."

Then where was Ben Clayton's room?

I said, "Then you take no stock in Mrs. Warren's psychic powers?"

Shutters seemed to come down in her dark eyes. Then she shrugged. "Sometimes I think it's mostly nonsense. But she had done some remarkable things. For instance, she told me how to recover a valuable diamond bracelet."

36

"You'd lost it?"

Her voice was cold. "It had been stolen from the top of my dressing table, where I was fool enough to leave it. Amy told me who the thief was. And she was right."

I recalled Kevin saying, "She finds out things about people. I don't know how, but she does."

"Mrs. Warren mentioned at dinner that there have been trespassers on the island."

My aunt looked away from me toward the opposite wall. For the first time since I had come into this room, I saw in her face evidence of the "strain" Amy Warren had mentioned. Her dark eyes brooded now, and lines at the corners of her mouth suddenly seemed more pronounced. Is she, I wondered incredulously, afraid of something? Perhaps because my childhood impression of her as an all-powerful figure still lingered, I found it hard to imagine her being afraid.

When she spoke, her voice sounded quite normal. "Yes, there have been trespassers. Kevin says it would be almost impossible to keep them off an island this close to shore, especially these days, when every Tom, Dick, and Harry has at least an outboard motorboat. Maybe he's right. But I didn't like it, so I bought a pair of Dobermans. I figured that with the dogs roaming the woods at night, I'd have no more uninvited visitors. But then the Dobermans got hold of poison somewhere."

I said, after a moment, "Did that happen after Mrs. Warren came here?"

The amused shine had returned to her eyes. "Yes. But don't think Amy poisoned them. She was the only one who made friends with those vicious brutes. With her they were as affectionate as cocker spaniels."

And the Dobermans' strange behavior, I reflected, must have reinforced whatever belief my aunt had in Amy Warren's powers as a "white witch." Just how strong was that belief? Strong enough that she would think the presence of that chattering woman might be some sort of protection?

It seemed to me inconsistent with my aunt's character that she should grant any credence at all to Mrs. Warren's claims. But then, how much did I know of my aunt's character? Only my childhood impressions of her and, in the last sixteen years, the impression conveyed by her infrequent cards and letters.

She broke in on my thoughts. "What did Madge think of my marriage? Was she surprised?"

"A little." I paused. "I saw your stepdaughter today. She's very beautiful."

"My stepdaughter!"

"Why—why, yes. Lisa Clayton. She was riding a bicycle down the road toward the gate."

"I agree that Lisa is beautiful. But she is not my stepdaughter."

I said, utterly at sea, "But isn't she Ben Clayton's daughter?"

"That's right. But what gave you the idea I was married to Ben Clayton?"

I said, beginning to feel angry, "Why, your letter. You said that you had married Ben Clayton last March."

I could tell that she was enjoying my confusion. "My letter didn't say that. It said that I had married, and that my name was now Clayton." She picked up her cigarette pack, shook it, and then crumpled it in her hand. "Jennifer, will you get me another pack of cigarettes?

There's a carton in the middle drawer of the highboy. Oh, and there's a key to the front door lying on top. That's yours."

I rose and moved across the room to the mahogany chest, noting automatically that it was American Chippendale. A brass candlestick nearly two feet high stood on its gleaming top. There was a Yale key there, too. I dropped the key in my pocket, opened the middle drawer, and extracted a pack of cigarettes from a carton. I walked back to her, held the lighter to her cigarette, and then sat down again.

"Thanks." Then, as someone knocked: "Come in."

The door opened. The blond man who had opened the gate for me that afternoon stood in the doorway. He wore a shirt now, a blue denim one, its sleeves rolled high on his muscular arms. He didn't look at me.

"Well, come on in, Harley." He moved across the room to stand at the foot of the bed. "Jennifer, this is my husband, Harley Clayton. Harley, this is my niece, Jennifer Langley."

He looked at me then and nodded. His blue eyes said clearly, "I know exactly what you're thinking, and to hell with you."

I managed to say, returning his gaze, "Mr. Clayton and I have already met."

He did not acknowledge that. Instead he looked at my aunt and said, "The riding mower may not be fixed by tomorrow. Kevin says the blades and the housing are bent."

"All right. We'll use the small power mower for now."

He nodded. "Well, good night." He turned and walked out of the room, closing the door behind him.

Five

"Shocked?" Aunt Evelyn asked.

I would not admit to that. "I'm surprised. After all, Mother and I just assumed you were married to Harley Clayton's father. Ben Clayton is his father, isn't he?"

"Was. Ben died several years ago. He picked up some sort of food poisoning in a restaurant."

She paused, and then went on, "I think you are shocked, and more than a little disappointed. Harley opened the gate for you this afternoon, didn't he? And you found him attractive."

I said coldly, "I noticed he was good-looking, if that's what you mean."

She laughed. "Well, feel free. Ours is strictly a marriage of convenience. In fact, he lives in the caretaker's cottage."

"Is that what he was before you married him, the caretaker?"

"That's what he still is."

When I did not speak, she went on, "I suppose you

want to know my reason for marrying him."

"Not particularly."

She studied my face for a second or two, and then laughed again. "My! He did get to you, didn't he? Well, I'll tell you the reason anyway. I felt that I, and this house, and this island, needed protection. More protection than I could get from a crippled war veteran."

"You make Kevin sound like a basket case. All he has is a limp."

She did not answer, but her smile told me she knew it was not just her reference to Kevin's handicap which had annoyed me.

The reason she had given for her marriage, I reflected, was obviously insufficient. True, perhaps she welcomed the protection of a husky man. But she'd had that as soon as she had hired him as caretaker.

Well, at least his reason for marrying her was clear. It was the reason for which any handsome young man marries a rich woman a generation older than himself.

I said, "If you don't mind, I think I'll go to bed."

"But I'd like for you to start on the inventory tomorrow, and we haven't even discussed what I'm to pay you. I'd like to offer you the equivalent of your salary in that antique shop."

Before I came here, I had intended to decline payment for my work. But now I felt differently about it. "I'm on salary plus commission. Lately, it's averaged out to about a hundred and eighty a week."

"Then that's what I'll pay you."

"Very well." That is, I added mentally, if I decide to stay here.

"I didn't know just what you'd need for your inventory, but I did ask Mrs. Escobar to put several ledgers in the library desk."

I nodded. "Can I do anything for you before I leave?"

"No. I'll ring for Mrs. Escobar after a while. That reminds me. She serves breakfast and lunch buffet style in the dining room. Breakfast is from seven o'clock on, and lunch is at one."

Again I nodded. "Well," I said, rising from my chair, "I'll say good night."

Halfway to the door I stopped and turned around, unable to resist the question. "By the way, was your husband in the Vietnam War, too?"

"He was a bomber pilot. He was drafted after he graduated from Florida U. seven years ago."

College graduate. Bomber pilot. Caretaker. And now a rich woman's husband. The sort of career you might call checkered.

"Well, good night, Aunt Evelyn."

Six

As I emerged into the hall, I looked to my left and saw Lisa Clayton step onto the stair landing. She still wore chinos and the sleeveless T-shirt. She looked at me, face impassive in its frame of gleaming hair, and gave a brief nod. Then she crossed to a door directly opposite the stairwell. She went into the room, closing the door behind her.

So, I thought, as I passed her door, Harley Clayton, despite his legal status, had been consigned to the caretaker's cottage. But his sister dwelt beneath the manorial roof. Then I realized that the tiny cottage probably did not have space for more than one person.

I went into my room, switched on the overhead light, and then switched it off. I crossed the room to stand at the eastern window, looking out. The light of a half moon silvered the side lawn. Beyond it stood the close-packed pines and hardwoods, black against the deep blue sky.

I did not like my Aunt Evelyn, I thought. I did not

like her at all. Should I tell her in the morning that I had decided to leave?

Immediately I began to think of reasons for staying. One, I had spent time and money coming down here. Two, because I had received no salary since the Unicorn Shop closed its door the final week in June, I could well use the money Aunt Evelyn offered. Three, my friend had been overwhelmed with joy at the prospect of living in my apartment for a month, and would be disappointed indeed if I ousted her after only a couple of days. Four, my mother and I had a vested interest in those valuables I had come down here to inventory. Despite my aunt's strange marriage, there was still a good chance that my mother and I would be the chief heirs to my grandfather's property.

But I knew that I had still another reason for wanting to stay, at least for a few days. It would be hard to walk out on so many unanswered questions. I wondered why Kevin had chosen to return to this island. I wondered at the unease I had glimpsed beneath my aunt's air of amused arrogance. As for Mrs. Warren, I never before had met any sort of witch, let alone one who looked like everybody's Aunt Amy.

Above all, I wondered about Harley Clayton, bomber pilot turned kept husband—and a very odd keptee, come to think of it, since I had first seen him, not driving a Ferrari or exercising a polo pony, but hammering a shingle onto a roof.

I glanced at the luminous dial of my watch. Almost eleven, and I felt as wide awake as if it were noon. I thought of how I used to lie awake in this house, apprehensively waiting for Aunt Evelyn to open my door a second time, and imagining behind my tightly closed eyelids what it would be like to run free in the moonlit world outside.

Well, there was moonlight tonight. And Aunt Evelyn, with one leg held by that contraption, could not prevent my going out, even if she had a mind to. Nor was I afraid to go out. The Dobermans were dead. And I did not fear trespassers—some pair of lovers who might come ashore off a small boat, or some group of teen-agers who would leave their moonlight-picnic spot strewn with beer cans. As a New Yorker, I felt that my two-block walk from the subway stop through the early dark on winter evenings held far more perils than I was likely to encounter on this island.

Nevertheless, I hesitated after I had switched on the light. Then, smiling a little at myself, I emptied my shoulder bag of most of its paraphernalia, and put in its place the New York girl's secret weapon against stray dogs, rapists, and muggers—a small can of hair spray.

As I moved down the staircase toward the dimly lighted lower hall, I had a sense of daring. That was absurd, I knew. Who cared now whether I left my room? Nevertheless, the feeling was there, and I found it exhilarating.

I unlocked the front door, relocked it behind me. Despite the fact that no breeze stirred the humid air, I caught the scent of the open sea about a mile away. I skirted the corner of the house and moved onto the east lawn. A long rectangle of bluish light fell from a ground floor window onto the grass. Glancing through the thin window curtain, I saw Mrs. Escobar and her plump niece seated before a TV set. I could not make out the tiny figures on the screen, but I could hear the muffled sound of gunfire and galloping hooves. From

45

the rear of the house came another sound, a banging of metal against metal. Kevin, I thought, out in the old carriage house, trying to straighten out the lawn mower's blades. Turning, I struck across the lawn toward a remembered gravel path through the trees.

The path was still there, and wider than it had been sixteen years before—so wide that moonlight fell upon the gravel, and I had no need for the small flashlight in my shoulder bag. Now and then a slight break in the trees walling the path indicated another path leading off to the right or left. It was hot there, with the walls of pines and live oaks making the air closer than ever. I hurried forward over rising ground, eager to reach the beach and the moonlit sea.

Then, when I could already hear the gentle wash of breakers on the beach, I paused at a branching path, memory stirring. Yes, there it was in its clearing off to my right, its concrete pillars blue-white in the moonlight. I turned toward it, and then stopped at the clearing's edge.

As a child I had never speculated about the age of that summerhouse, a rectangular structure built in the shape of a small Greek temple, its pillared sides open to the weather. But now I knew that it must be younger than the main house. Probably it had been built around 1830, when the English craze for classic and medieval replicas had crossed the Atlantic, and rich Americans, too, began to ornament their estates with Greek temples, miniature fourteenth-century castles, and artfully strewn "ruins."

To my seven-year-old eyes that summerhouse had seemed fascinating, and far more beautiful than the main house. Now this attempt of some long-dead person to invoke a bit of classical Greece in mortar, here in this subtropical woodland, looked absurd. But I still liked its situation, there at the foot of a low limestone bluff, thickly wooded, which rose on the island's seaward side. There was a spring in the low hillside, I recalled now, its water trickling down to sink into the soft sand at the bluff's base.

Had there been grass in this clearing sixteen years ago? I could not remember. But if so, it had been replaced by a tangle of vines, seedling oaks, and what looked in this uncertain light to be wild azaleas, blossomless now. There was still a discernible path through the tangle. I went up it, mounted two low steps, and moved through the doorway beneath the triangular pediment. The pavilion's floor, paved inappropriately with gray slate cut into rectangular flagstones, lay striped by alternate swaths of moonlight and the pillars' shadows.

There must have been some sort of seating arrangement in this summerhouse a hundred years ago or more. But now the building stood as I had first seen it, empty except for a series of stone lions' heads, each with an iron ring in its mouth, affixed to the pillars on the eastern side, and a two-foot-high bronze cherub, standing with cupped hands in a bronze basin near one of the pillars. I could make out his dim form in the pillar's shadow.

And then, feeling chilled, I grasped the memory which had eluded me when Kevin came into my room before dinner.

Aunt Evelyn had left the house that afternoon sixteen years ago. From my window under the starlings' nesting site, I had watched as, dark hair wrapped in a yellow chiffon scarf, she had driven her red convertible along the road leading to the gate. Then I had turned sadly to my jigsaw puzzles and my books, regretting for not the first time that I had mentioned to my aunt that my father, starting when I was not yet five, had taught me how to read. Since I could read, she had announced my second day under her roof, I would devote my afternoons to the books I had brought with me. I could also work the jigsaw puzzles she would supply. As for fresh air, outdoor play in the mornings would afford me enough of that.

Perhaps an hour later I was plodding through the third—and drearily familiar—chapter of *Five Little Peppers,* when I heard gravel rattle against the screen. Abandoning Mrs. Pepper and her repulsively well-behaved brood, I ran to the window. Kevin stood down there on the drive. Cupping his hands to his mouth, he called softly, "Come on down. I've got something to show you."

Flattered by an invitation from this twelve-year-old who so often ignored me, I slipped out of my room. I went down the stairs very quietly, lest Mrs. Shaughnessy hear. She was my friend, but nevertheless she would feel duty-bound to report me, especially since it was her son who was leading me into disobedience.

When I was outside, I followed Kevin along the path through the still, humid woodland, and then along the branching path to the pavilion. In its doorway I stood rooted, overcome with delight and admiration.

I had not realized that the cherub was a fountain, but it was, and Kevin had set it going. Water spilled from the laughing mouth into the cupped hands, and from there into the basin. With a casual air that did

48

not hide his pride, he explained his handiwork to me.

In the pavilion's early days a metal pipe must have led from the hillside spring through a hole in one pillar, a hole I had not noticed before, and from there into the small bronze head. In place of a pipe, Kevin had used a long length of green garden hose. He had attached another length of hose to a discharge hole in the basin, thus leading the water between two pillars to the sandy earth outside.

I had watched the wonderful fountain for at least two minutes when I became aware of small chips of mortar strewn on the flagstones around the basin, and of a coil of rope lying several feet away. "What's all that?" I asked.

"Nothing. I was just fooling around. You know how I rigged the hose up at the spring? I got this funnel from the kitchen, see, and I stuck the end of it in the hose and wrapped wire around it, tight. Then I anchored the whole thing with more wire to a couple of bushes, so that the funnel's mouth is right under where the water comes out. Come on. I'll show you."

We turned around. Aunt Evelyn stood in the doorway. She wore a yellow shirt, and brown pedal pushers that stopped midway of her sun-tanned calves. The yellow scarf still covered her dark hair. Smiling, she walked over to us and looked at the marvelous fountain and the mortar chips on the floor. "That garden hose you cut will come out of your mother's wages."

She still had that smile, and it made her more frightening than a scowl would have. "Now clean this mess up. And if you ever do anything like this again, I'll fire your mother. Do you know how old your mother is?"

49

Kevin did not answer.

"Your mother is fifty. How many people will hire a fifty-year-old housekeeper with a boy, especially a sneaky, destructive boy like you? She'd have to go on relief. How would you like that, the relief people coming each month to some dingy room you'll have somewhere to ask your mother a lot of questions?" She paused. "Well?"

Kevin's face looked tight over the cheekbones, and so white that his freckles seemed to stand out. In my own cringing stomach I could feel his humiliation and fear. He muttered, "I wouldn't like it."

"All right then. Just remember." She looked at me. "You and I are going back to the house, Jennifer."

I don't remember walking with her back to the house. But I do remember my punishment. She deprived me for three days of those jigsaw puzzles she had furnished. I didn't mind. I had come to loathe them, and I never touch jigsaw puzzles, even now.

I stood there in the moonlit doorway, wondering again at the grown-up Kevin's presence on this island. Then I turned away, rejoined the main path, and followed it to where steps, carved in the limestone bluff, led down to the beach.

Except for the ragged white lines of low breakers, the Atlantic lay calm in the moonlight, a darker blue beneath the dark blue sky. Low on the southeastern horizon the Archer aimed his bow, and overhead the Swan and the Eagle flew in opposite directions, their brilliance dimmed by the moonlight. Feeling the humid warmth press down, I suddenly longed for the caress of tropical water, and wished I had worn a bathing suit under my dress. Should I go swimming anyway? No; at any moment some power boat might come chugging around the island's end.

At last I was beginning to feel sleepy. For a few minutes longer I stood there, my gaze following the lights of some slow-moving ship several miles offshore. Then I turned, climbed the limestone steps, and started back along the path.

Footsteps, crunching toward me over the gravel. I halted, trying to control a sudden leap of alarm. It was only Kevin, probably. As a boy he had loved the sea. But if it was not Kevin?

Before I left the house, I had decided that the only trespassers I would be apt to meet would be some amorous couple or a group of adventurous teen-agers. But it was only one person who moved toward me with lengthy, masculine strides. And I was a long way from the house. Remembering that odd dinner conversation, remembering the unease in my aunt's face, I decided not to take any chances. Quickly I stepped off the path, hoping that no twig would snap underfoot, and retreated beyond the first line of trees.

The footsteps had slowed. Had he heard my own footsteps or caught a glimpse of me before I turned off the path? If so, he was not Kevin. Kevin would have called out to me.

Through the screen of leaves I saw a man come to a halt almost directly opposite me. The moonlight was bright enough to show me that I had never seen him before. Heartbeats heavy now, I noticed that he was a slender man, above medium height, wearing dark trousers and a short-sleeved sport shirt. For a tense moment I expected him to turn toward me. Then I saw him place a cigarette between his lips.

I heard the click of a lighter, saw it flare, go out. He lit it again and held it to his cigarette for a second or two. Then he walked on.

But I still stood there, feeling cold despite the night's warmth. The face revealed by the lighter's flame had been that of a man in his early thirties, dark-haired, olive-skinned, hawk-nosed, and with a whitish scar slanting from his left temple to the corner of his mouth. Useless to tell myself that it was the scar which had conveyed that impression of evil. I felt sure that the man *was* evil. And like a coiled snake, the sight of him had brought me repulsion as well as fear.

The crunch of his withdrawing footsteps had ceased. I strained my ears, hoping to hear him descend the limestone steps to the beach, but there was no sound. Evidently he stood at the top of the steps, smoking his cigarette and looking out over the water. I fought down the impulse to dart from my hiding place and run toward the house. He would surely hear me and turn around. And if he chose to, he could overtake me long before I reached the house.

Although it seemed like half an hour, probably not more than five minutes went by before I heard his returning footsteps. They did not slacken as he passed by beyond the screen of leaves. The crunching gradually died away.

It was not until then that I remembered the can of hair spray. I took the metal cylinder from my shoulder bag and held it in my hand. I stood listening for another few seconds and then, hearing only the lazy wash of surf, I stepped onto the path and moved at a half run toward the house. He was well away from here by now. The evidence of my ears had told me that. It was absurd to feel that any moment he might step onto the path behind me and clap a hand over my mouth.

When I reached the path leading to the pavilion, I threw a glance down it. Could he have gone in there? Of course. But also he could have struck off into any of the dim paths leading north and south from this one. I hurried on, beginning to feel winded now, and painfully conscious of a pebble lodged in my shoe.

When I reached the clearing around the house, I saw that light still spilled from the old carriage house onto the back lawn. Kevin, evidently, still worked on the damaged mower blade. I moved several yards onto the side lawn, well away from the trees behind me, and stopped to shake the pebble from my shoe. Then I walked on, past the stairs slanting up the eastern wall of the house to the second-floor balcony in the rear. Glancing up, I saw dim, bluish light shining through the partially closed draperies of my aunt's corner room. A TV set? Some sort of night light? I moved on across the graveled space in front of the carriage house.

The door to the section which, sixteen years ago at least, had held two horse stalls was closed. But through the raised door of the other section I could see light beating down on a dark green Lincoln Continental sedan, undoubtedly Aunt Evelyn's, and a battered MG that was probably Kevin's, and on my own little bug. Kevin stood at a broad workbench which held the mower's detached blades. He was frowning as he ran a finger along one of the steel edges.

At the sound of my footsteps he turned, a surprised look on his face. "Hi, night owl." Then, with his gaze dropping to my left hand: "Thanks, but all I use on my hair is a little bear grease."

53

"Oh!" I hadn't realized I still held the can of hair spray. As I restored it to my shoulder bag, Kevin asked, in an altered tone, "What's the matter?"

I told him. He said, "I thought I heard a power boat start up about five or ten minutes ago.

"There's a dock at the island's northern end," he went on. "Keep-off signs are plastered all over it, and there's a locked wooden gate at the seaward end, but that doesn't keep people off if they're determined to get on."

"But who could he have been?"

"If he was as shady-looking as you say, I'd guess his native turf was Havana." Then, at my dubious look: "Oh, I know. Most of the Cuban refugees have been business and professional people, plus a few farmers and working people. But some really tough characters, too, put blue water between themselves and Castro. Ask anyone in Miami. There's a real Cuban Mafia down there."

"But why should he come here?"

Kevin shrugged. "Who knows? But even mobsters behave like the rest of us much of the time. They watch football on TV, eat hamburgers, and drive power boats. And they pay no attention to no-trespassing signs. Maybe he just wanted to explore. Maybe he likes to stand on a bluff and look south and east to his old stamping ground. One thing's sure. If he had come here to case the house for burglary, he wouldn't have strolled casually down to the beach nearly a mile away."

"I suppose you're right."

Here in this garage with its flooding fluorescent light and its smell of oil and grease, my alarm had ebbed. Oh, I still felt that the man I had seen was essentially evil. But probably it had been no evil intent which had brought him to the island tonight.

"Just the same," Kevin said, "I'll look over the island tomorrow. Maybe it would help to string barbed wire over that gate at the end of the dock. And I'll phone that kennel in St. Augustine to see if they can hurry up with the Dobermans. We're to get a new pair as soon as they've finished their training course."

"Don't hurry on my account. I'd be more afraid of the Dobermans than any number of trespassers."

He grinned. "Can't say that I blame you." Then, after a pause: "Going to tell your aunt about that man you saw tonight?"

"Should I?"

"Up to you."

I said slowly, "I don't know whether I should or not. She seems a bit jumpy as it is."

"I know. Maybe it's Amy Warren's spooky patter. Then again, maybe not. Your aunt has lived"—he hesitated, as if searching for the word—"a very interesting life. Maybe now in her middle age she's coming unstrung."

He paused. "Know who her husband is now?"

I felt color in my face. "Yes. You should have told me."

"Sorry about that. I couldn't resist letting you find out for yourself."

To keep him from pursuing the subject, I asked, "Are you going to work on those blades all night?"

"No, I ought to have them fixed soon. I'm stubborn that way. If I see something that doesn't work, I have to keep tinkering until it does."

Just as he had made the fountain work. But never

would I remind him of those moments when he had stood there, white-faced with fear and humiliation.

He said, "If I can't get it right in another half hour, though, I'll go to bed."

"In the house? Do you have sleeping as well as dining privileges?"

"Sure. My room's on the opposite side of the hall from yours, two doors toward the west. If a bogeyman climbs in your window, call me and I'll throw him out. Unless," he added, "it's me climbing in."

I laughed. "See you in the morning," I said, and turned away.

Seven

When I reached the stairs slanting up the eastern wall of the house, I hesitated. After all, this island belonged to my aunt. She might be justifiably annoyed if I did not tell her promptly about the stranger I had seen. On the other hand, if she were asleep, if the dim glow I had seen came from a night light, certainly I should not awaken her. The best thing, I decided, would be to walk along the balcony to those partially drawn draperies. If I could see that she was awake, I would knock. Otherwise I would wait until the next time I saw her.

I climbed the stairs. As I moved along the balcony, past the darkened windows, past a table and chair of white wicker, I heard no murmuring TV set. Evidently that bluish glow, shining out onto the balcony rail and onto the limb of a giant live oak that extended toward it, came from a night light.

Yes, evidently she had fallen asleep without first calling Mrs. Escobar to help her undress. Through the gap in the draperies I could see the foot of the white iron bed. She lay motionless, still in the blue kaftan, atop the coverlet, her right leg imprisoned by the traction sling.

I started to turn away, and then halted. She was not alone in there. Someone had begun to speak in a low, rhythmical voice. After a moment I realized to whom the voice belonged. Amy Warren. Amy, somewhere outside the line of my vision, sitting or standing in the bluish glow and chanting unintelligible words—words that did not seem to belong to any language I had ever heard.

I felt my scalp prickle.

She was a follower of the Old Religion, she had said. Thousands of years ago, had some priestess chanted those words in some sacred forest in Gaul, or to ancient Britons who had toiled up the hill through the pre-dawn darkness to the Circle of Stones?

The chanting stopped.

For a second or two there was no sound at all. And then it came out of nowhere, a wind that rattled the leaves in the live oak behind me, and struck through my thin dress.

Sweat sprang out on my palms and upper lip—sweat that felt cold in that sudden rush of air. Then, as abruptly as it had sprung up, the wind ceased, and the night was as silent and humid as before.

On even the calmest night, a wind might come out of nowhere. Of course it might. No reason to stand here, rooted to the spot, with chills rippling down my body.

I heard Amy's voice, oddly hushed, but no longer cadenced. "The guardian power is here now. It is all around you. Nothing vengeful can get through to you."

Silence for a moment. Then my aunt said, "But I can feel him in this house."

"Right now, dear?"

"No, not right now. But last night I felt he was here. It was very late, two or three in the morning, I guess. I could feel him out there in the hall, right outside my door, where I caught a glimpse of him that once."

"But don't you see, dear? He hasn't manifested himself since I have been in this house. And that is because my power is so much stronger than his."

My aunt went on, as if the other woman hadn't spoken, "And when I did get to sleep, I had more of those damned dreams. I tell you, Amy, I'm afraid, and that makes me furious, because never in my life have I been afraid of man, woman, or child."

"They're only dreams, dear."

When my aunt finally answered, her voice had turned cold. "Only dreams. Not real, you mean."

"Now, Evelyn . . ." Amy's voice was apprehensive.

"And maybe when I climbed the stairs that night last fall and looked down the hall, I didn't really see him standing there, not even for a second or two. Maybe my eyes were playing tricks on me. Or my mind. In that case, I need an oculist or a head shrinker, not some chattering woman from Nebraska."

"Evelyn! Let me remind you that you *invited* me to stay in your house—"

"Maybe you're just playing me for a sucker."

"Evelyn, whenever you talk like this, I get half a mind to pack my things and leave. I really do. If it wasn't that I know you need my protection—"

"Protection! Half the time I think that you're a ridiculous fake, and I'm just a damn fool who thought she

59

saw a ghost one night."

"Let me remind you that it was because you saw it that you struck up an acquaintance with me. I didn't speak to *you* that day under the dryers, *you* spoke to—"

"As for your packing your things, I'll believe that when I see it. You know when you're sitting in a tub of butter."

"Evelyn!" Amy's voice held dignified pain. "If after all I've done for you, you begrudge me a room here and the little bit of food I eat—"

I was able to turn away then. They had become just two middle-aged women, squabbling in the night. Swiftly and quietly I retraced my steps along the balcony.

Nothing vengeful can get through to you, Amy had said. Just who was it my aunt had seen, or thought she had seen, standing outside her bedroom door one night months ago? Well, no doubt Kevin had been right about her having led an "interesting" life, almost a half century of it. During that time many people, some still living, some now dead, must have had reason to feel vengeful toward Evelyn Dunway Clayton.

Well, thank Heaven, it was no concern of mine. And even though, when the wind had rattled the oak leaves, I had felt chilled for a few moments by something more than the wind itself, I still took little stock in Amy Warren's powers, and even less in a shadowy figure which my aunt sometimes believed, and sometimes doubted, that she had seen in this house.

But at least I knew now why her face had taken on that haggard look when I mentioned trespassers. The word must have brought to mind, not just living invaders, but one who, if he existed, could not be kept out

60

by fences, locks, or even guard dogs.

I glanced toward the garage. No light there now. Evidently Kevin had gone to bed. I descended the stairs through the humid silence and went around the corner of the house to the front door.

Eight

I slept late the next morning. When I came into the dining room around nine-thirty, only Amy Warren sat at the long table, wearing the same print dress she had worn the night before. She looked up from her tomato juice and dry toast to say brightly, "Hello, sleepyhead."

That middle-western voice, that dowdy dress. Hard to believe I had heard her chanting in that room dimly illuminated by a blue light. Had she and my aunt made up their quarrel? Apparently. Amy did not have the look of a woman about to "pack her things." Probably, I reflected, they quarreled whenever the needle of my aunt's emotional compass swung to cynical disbelief, and then made it up when the needle swung back to credulity, or to an amused tolerance of the woman who, even though she might be a fraud, was still "a barrel of laughs."

"Good morning." I helped myself to scrambled eggs, sausage, and toast from the buffet, and then sat down opposite her.

Looking at my plate, she sighed. "I used to be able to eat like that, but now everything goes to my hips."

"Well, I'm unusually hungry this morning."

"Probably because you slept so late. And I don't wonder at that. Around midnight I heard voices, and so I looked out and saw you and Kevin in the garage."

That must have been, I reflected, just before she moved through the connecting bath to my aunt's room, dimly illuminated by the night light. "I'm sorry we disturbed you."

"Oh, I hadn't gone to sleep yet. But, Jennifer—may I call you Jennifer?"

"Of course."

"Good. And I'm Amy. Jennifer, I think I ought to warn you about that young man."

What did she want to tell me? That he smoked marijuana? That in St. Augustine he associated with girls of a type a man does not take home to meet Mother? "I don't think you have to warn me about Kevin. I knew him when we were both children."

"Evelyn mentioned that. But people can change a lot as they grow up. And Kevin Shaughnessy grew up to be a liar. That limp of his. That's not a battle wound. He was shot in the leg during some sort of brawl in a Saigon bar."

"Did he tell you that?"

"Of course not."

"Then how do you know?"

"Don't worry, I know."

I thought of how Kevin himself had said that Amy seemed to have ways of finding out things. I said, "Assuming you're right, don't you think you should tell my aunt?"

"I did, but she brushed it aside. Evelyn's too soft, too generous."

I looked at her to see if she were joking. She did not appear to be. Well, perhaps much of the time she was able to persuade herself to see her rich friend in that rosy light. I said, "Perhaps my aunt thought it was Kevin's business. Frankly, I do, too."

"Oh, my dear! I just thought I ought to warn you. After all, you're very young."

"Not very. I'm twenty-three."

"As old as that? I guess by the time you're my age everyone under twenty-five looks like a schoolgirl." She paused. "Do you live alone in New York?"

"Yes, I have an apartment."

"A large one?"

"No." I felt tempted to add, "It's just the right size for staging quiet little orgies."

"Well," she said, pushing back her chair, "I'd better go upstairs. I want to write some letters this morning."

"How do you mail letters here?"

"Harley does it. He goes over to the post office in Galton Beach each morning."

I wondered what she thought of my aunt's young husband. But even if I had felt inclined to discuss him with her, I doubted that she would tell me what she really thought—not when it might get back to Aunt Evelyn.

She left me then. I finished my eggs and sausage, had a second cup of coffee, and then went into the library. The shrubbery that crowded close to the house was especially dense here, so that little daylight came through the long windows. I touched a switch. Light blazed down from a chandelier of Waterford crystal, glittering on the gold-tooled bindings of books that lined one wall, and on the glass of various display cases that lined the other three.

I moved slowly from one display case to another. Flanking a tall secretary desk were two étagères, one holding highly polished seashells, and the other an array of snuffboxes made of about every conceivable material from silver and gold to onyx and enamel. There were two flat display cases of coins, and two cases of miniatures, many with jeweled frames, and some of them obviously dating back to the early eighteenth century. What had my grandfather felt when he looked at these small portraits of white-wigged men and women? Envy of those serenely arrogant faces? Or pride that he, a sharecropper's son, could buy these portraits for which dukes and countesses had sat?

Each case was padlocked. Where were the keys? Well, no matter. I would not start with the collections. I knew a little about miniatures, practically nothing about coins, and nothing at all about seashells. Better to start with china and glassware, which I did know something about.

I was taking a ledger from the desk drawer when I became aware that someone had entered the room. I turned. Lisa Clayton stood there at the end of the long library table, blond hair shining in the chandelier's light. Today she wore a pink cotton shirt and white shorts that exposed about a yard of smooth, golden-tan legs.

I said, smiling, "Hello."

She nodded. "How long are you going to be here?"

Even though I was almost sure what she meant, I asked, "In the library? I was just leaving."

"I mean here on the island."

Her words and tone were almost childishly rude. But there was nothing childlike about the cool, appraising hostility in her gray eyes.

I felt an answering hostility. "I'll be here until I've finished my inventory of the valuables in this house. That's what I came here for, you know."

"Yes, I heard." She paused. "But I should think you'd be terribly bored down here."

"Why? Are you bored?"

"No, but I grew up in Florida. I'd hate living where I couldn't swim and water ski all year round. But you're a New Yorker. I should think you'd miss all the night spots and Broadway shows and so on."

"Believe it or not, millions of New Yorkers go to bed at ten o'clock five nights a week, seldom see a play, and have never set foot in Twenty-one."

"You didn't go to bed last night at ten. I saw you out in the garage with Kevin."

I recalled then that her room overlooked the rear lawn, like Aunt Evelyn's and Amy's. And Kevin's.

Perhaps Kevin was the reason she wanted me to leave. I said, in a friendlier tone, "Yes, I was telling him about this man I'd seen walking down to the beach."

"I know. Kevin told me. If you're going to panic every time you see a trespasser, you're not going to be very happy here."

She had riled me again. "Where is the best china and glassware kept?"

"In a room near the kitchen, I think. Ask Mrs. Escobar."

I turned back to the desk, took a sharpened yellow

66

pencil from the drawer, and started toward the doorway. Lisa said, "You didn't tell me how long you'll be staying here."

I halted. "Yes, I did. Until the inventory's finished."

"But how long will that be?"

"Oh, maybe a year."

At the look of consternation in her face, I relented. After all, she was at least four years younger than myself, perhaps five. And if the trouble was Kevin—well, in a way it was both touching and flattering to think that a girl so beautiful would be jealous of me.

"I was kidding," I said. "I'll be here a month at most, and I'll leave even sooner, if possible. You see," I lied, "there's a special man in New York I want to get back to."

She relaxed visibly, and almost smiled. "You'd better do that. You can't keep a man on ice."

"How true. Well, see you."

I crossed the dining room and then stopped in the archway to the hall. Dr. Satherly, black bag in hand, was starting up the stairs. He turned his head to look at me, and then paused. His thin mouth looked even more pinched than it had the night before.

I said, "Good morning. Is something wrong with Aunt Evelyn?"

"No. She phoned me that she's read a magazine article about vitamin pills. She wants me to read it, too, and tell her what I think."

No wonder he looked peevish. He had seen her yesterday, after dinner as well as in the afternoon, and now she had summoned him back to read an article she could just as easily have mailed to him. I wondered that he would permit such a waste of his time, no matter

67

how much she paid him. He nodded to me and went up the stairs.

I walked back to the hall which ran along the rear of the house, and turned right, looking for a vaguely remembered pair of green baize doors. I found them, pushed them open, and stopped just inside the big, immaculately clean kitchen. "Good morning."

Mrs. Escobar, stirring the contents of a black enamel pot that stood on the big electric range, gave me a surprised but friendly smile. Lorena, seated at a long Formica-topped table, also smiled at me and then, with a frown of concentration, resumed peeling a large potato.

"Forgive the intrusion," I said, and explained why I was there.

"The best china and glassware is in a room across the hall," Mrs. Escobar told me. "It is seldom used. Some of it is on high shelves. Lorena will help you. She is very careful."

Turning to her niece, she spoke in rapid Spanish. Lorena smiled at me and laid down the paring knife. She crossed the room to the long stainless steel sink and picked up the aluminum stepladder that stood beside it.

I followed her across the hall. Opening a door, she reached inside to switch on the light, and then stepped back for me to enter. Along the rear wall, a cabinet of cut glass—tumblers and punch bowls and flower vases and platters of every size—made an iridescent dazzle. On the right- and left-hand walls, even larger glass-doored cabinets held china. A long, felt-covered table ran down the center of the room.

With a gesture, I conveyed to Lorena that we would start with the top shelf of one of the china cabinets.

Standing on the ladder, she handed down piece after piece of a white Lennox dinner service, banded with gold. Just as carefully, I placed each piece on the table and entered it in my ledger. At last I asked, "Is that everything on the top shelf?" When she looked down at me with puzzled brown eyes, I fell back upon the small vocabulary I had retained from a one-year high school course in Spanish. "*Es todo?*"

She shook her head. Reaching far back onto the shelf, she brought out a small plate, looked at it, and handed it down to me. It was a child's earthenware plate, not especially valuable, except to a collector of such plates, but perhaps a hundred years old, and very charming. Painted on it was a small boy in a long-trousered sailor suit and a broad-brimmed hat with streamers, rolling a hoop. On the rim were the initials J.H.H. John Henry Haywood? James Howard?

Lorena had descended the ladder to stand beside me. "*Qué es?*"

"A little boy's plate. I mean, *es—para un niño.*"

Her face lighted up. "Ah! *Un niño.*" She smiled although her lower lip had begun to tremble. "*Tengo*—I have—*un niño.*"

"You have? Where is he?"

The plump face was distorted now. For a moment she looked at me silently, tears welling in her eyes. Then she said, "*No sé!*" and covered her face with her hands and began to sob.

"Oh, Lorena!"

I had my arms around her, trying to comfort her, when Mrs. Escobar came in, her face anxious. "What is it?"

"I don't know. Something about a little boy."

Sorrow came into her face. She put her hand on Lorena's heaving shoulder. *"Váyate,"* she said gently, and added something in Spanish too rapid for me to follow. Still sobbing, the girl went out of the room.

Mrs. Escobar said, into the silence, "I will tell you about it."

"You don't have to do that."

"I want to!" Her tone was vehement. "I don't want you to hear it from someone else. You are a nice girl—a nice young lady—and I want you to think well of us."

She explained then that although she herself had left Cuba six years ago, her sister and her sister's daughter had not come to the mainland until four years later. "They boarded with some other refugees in St. Augustine. I paid for their board out of my wages here. I was the only one who could work, you see. Lorena was too young to quit school, and my sister has bad heart trouble."

As soon as Lorena was seventeen, and legally able to seek work, she had come to the island as a housemaid. She had been here only a few weeks when Mrs. Escobar had discovered the girl was several months pregnant. As nearly as Mrs. Escobar and her sister could determine, the father was a young "Anglo"—native-born white American—who had been a classmate of Lorena's. However, he denied responsibility, and refused to marry her.

"I told Mrs. Clayton—Miss Dunway, she was then—about it. I told her Lorena wanted to have the baby. My niece is a good Catholic, as I am, and she loves children. And my sister had said she would take care of the baby. Miss Dunway said Lorena could work here until just before the baby was born, and have her job back later."

70

She paused, a look of challenge in her eyes, as if expecting me to comment that that had been darned nice of Aunt Evelyn. I did not. I was sure that generosity had not prompted her decision. Aunt Evelyn had been onto a good thing in these days when servants are hard to get—a strong, willing girl, sufficiently retarded not to be bored with her job in this isolated house.

The baby, "a handsome boy with red hair and gray eyes," had been born in a St. Augustine hospital. The second day after the child's birth, Dr. Satherly had brought Lorena a paper to sign.

"It was a paper which said she wanted to have the child adopted. But Lorena did not know that, of course. She just did what the doctor asked."

I said, appalled, "And the child was adopted? But couldn't you have stopped that? Couldn't you have gone to the adoption agency and explained to them—"

"There was no agency. The adoption was—how do you say it?—privately arranged."

"By Dr. Satherly?"

"Yes."

Privately arranged adoptions often brought the arranger considerable, and illegal, sums of money. If Dr. Satherly had come out of the deal many thousands richer, and my aunt knew about it, that might explain why she could command him to dance attendance upon her.

I said, furious, "How can the two of you go on working for her? Why don't you leave her flat, broken leg and all?"

Mrs. Escobar's smile held no amusement. "Both Lorena and I must work. Her mother's medicine is very expensive. And although Lorena works well as long as I am here to give her orders in Spanish, she would have a

71

hard time alone. Many weeks might pass before we found someone else to hire the both of us."

The bleak compulsions of the poor, I thought.

And then I thought of that woman lying in that up-stairs room. How to explain her? Oh, yes, I know Lord Acton's aphorism about power corrupting, and absolute power corrupting absolutely. But he said nothing about how the appetite for such power arises. How could it be that Evelyn Dunway Clayton and my soft-hearted—and sometimes soft-headed—mother could have grown up in the same environment?

But perhaps it was not the same emotional environ-ment. My mother had told me, almost without rancor, that she had always been aware that her father was quite besotted by his first-born child. Was that when Evelyn Dunway's appetite for power had awakened, when she discovered that she could wind her father around her little finger? Or was it when the boys began to flock around? Or was it still later when, as sole inher-itor of the island and my grandfather's money, she found herself ruler of a tiny kingdom?

Mrs. Escobar said, "Mrs. Clayton rang for me a few minutes ago. She wanted me to find you and give you a message. She would like to see you in her room after dinner."

I nodded.

"Lorena must have stopped crying by now. I will send her back to you."

"Please don't. I can use the stepladder."

"As you wish."

Nine

I had catalogued the contents of one china cupboard and started on the second, when I began to feel hungry. I went to my room, washed dust from my hands and face, and descended to the dining room. No one was there. The buffet still offered food, though—a silver platter of cold meats garnished with parsley, and a bowl of green salad.

Near the end of my solitary meal, I decided not to return to work immediately. First I would walk down to the beach. There was a limestone cave I wanted to see again. As a child I had taken the cave's existence for granted. But in a college geology class I had learned that although limestone is plentiful in Florida, underlying most of its inland lakes, limestone outcrops are rare along the southern part of the barrier beach, that series of islands strung from Maine to Key West.

I found the woods not only hotter than the night before, but noisier. Among the trees along both sides of the path, chattering squirrels hurtled from branch to branch, dislodging acorns. I could hear the screech of Florida jays, and once one of them, no doubt caught in some criminal enterprise, darted across the path a few feet ahead of me, hotly pursued by a yellow-breasted chat, its legs comically dangling as it flew.

At the branching path which led to the pavilion, I hesitated. But no. It was the beach and the cave I wanted to see. I moved on past the spot where I had left the path the night before and, through a screen of leaves, had seen a stranger's profile bent above a cigarette lighter. Despite Lisa's scornful words, I was not ashamed of the impulse which had led me to leave the path. Even now, in the midafternoon sunlight, I was sure that the man was not one with whom I would have wanted to exchange pleasantries, especially not at night and in an isolated spot.

At the top of the steps hewn into the bluff lay a cigarette stub, ground into brown shreds under someone's shoe. For a minute or so I stood looking out across the Atlantic. Except for its ruffled edging of low white waves, the sparkling sea looked almost as calm as a mountain lake. I descended the steps and turned to my right along the bluff.

The cave, when I reached it, looked shallower and less lofty than it had to my seven-year-old eyes. At some time when the island was lower than at present, pounding waves had carved out a cavern about eight feet high and twelve feet wide. The sandy floor, strewn with small rounded rocks, sloped gently upward about nine feet to the cave's curving rear wall. No doubt if the island had not risen a few feet, waves would have eaten even farther into the bluff. As it was, one spot in the rear wall about three feet above the sandy floor, evidently of weaker consistency than the rest, had begun to crumble into chunks of limestone, mingled with a few small rocks which, carried in by storm-driven waves, had lodged there.

Suddenly I recalled a morning when I had tagged after twelve-year-old Kevin down to the beach. It must have been only a few days after that fountain episode in the pavilion. Standing in almost the same spot where I now stood, I had watched him work with his hands and an old tire iron at that area of crumbling limestone. He was going to see, he explained to me impatiently over his shoulder, if there was another cave beyond. When the cave floor was littered with limestone fragments, he had thrust a hand in the small hole he had made. For a moment he stood motionless. Then he looked at me, face taut with excitement.

"There's something back there. It feels like iron."

We stared at each other. I knew that he, like me, was picturing a pirate's chest, crammed with rubies, diamonds, and golden doubloons. He started to move past me. "I'm going to get a crowbar."

"You'd better not. What if Aunt Evelyn catches you?"

He said nothing, just turned back into the cave and began to gather up the limestone fragments and cram them back into the small opening. From the pallor of his face I knew that he was picturing that dingy room somewhere, and a welfare lady asking his mother questions.

Had he on some later day tried to break through to that probably nonexistent pirate's chest? I thought not. My aunt's threat had been an effective one. Besides, an adolescent's interest shifts with bewildering speed.

75

Within a few months his former fascination with the cave might have seemed childish to him.

But I still liked to think of that morning. I stood there, recalling the excitement that had stirred in me at the thought of pirate treasure, until a metallic gleam in one corner of the cave caught my eye. Three beer cans and a crumpled plastic bag which probably had held potato chips.

If I ever climbed Mount Everest, which seemed unlikely, would I find beer cans up there? Probably.

Turning away, I started back toward the limestone steps. Then I halted.

Harley Clayton, in blue jeans and a blue denim shirt, was moving toward me along the beach. He carried a roll of barbed wire over one shoulder and a tool kit in one hand. When he was about fifteen yards away, he bent to pick up some object from the sand. He dropped it in his shirt pocket and walked on. After a moment's hesitation, I advanced to meet him.

"Hello," I said. "Beautiful day, isn't it?"

His unsmiling nod acknowledged that it was. I saw now that he had padded the roll of barbed wire with wrapped canvas at the point where it rested on his shoulder. I also saw, protruding above his shirt pocket, the pointed end of a pinkish seashell.

I said, "Have you been putting up a fence?"

"In a way. I strung wire across the gate at the end of the dock. Kevin thinks the man you saw last night may have landed there."

"So Kevin told you about that."

He made no answer to that brilliant piece of deduction. I tried another tack. "Did you know Kevin in Vietnam?"

76

"No. I made bombing runs off a carrier. He was stationed in Saigon."

"All the time? Wasn't he ever in combat?"

"I don't know. I don't talk about the war, not with him or anyone else."

It was a direct snub. But I, beginning to feel stubborn, persisted. "Amy Warren told me he got his limp in some sort of brawl in a Saigon bar."

"So? Why don't you ask Kevin about it?"

I felt warmth in my face. "I was hoping," I said with dignity, "that you would tell me that isn't true. You see, I like Kevin."

"Sorry. I can't tell you anything, one way or the other."

The silence lengthened embarrassingly. But still he did not turn away, and so I said, "What's the shell you picked up?"

"A *conus sozoni*." For the first time, his voice held a shade of animation. "You seldom find them this far north."

He reached into his pocket. I looked at the cone-shaped shell he held out on his big palm. Against its pale pink background, the shell was banded with stripes of warm brown. "It's beautiful," I said.

He did not answer. He was looking past my shoulder and out to sea. I turned, following the direction of his gaze. About a quarter of a mile offshore a line of pelicans flew, grotesque and yet graceful, pouched throats and chunky bodies black against the blue sky, wings moving slowly and majestically.

I counted. "Fourteen of them."

Harley said, "It's tragic, like watching dinosaurs." When I looked at him questioningly, he went on,

"Soon pelicans will be extinct. When I was a small boy, I sometimes counted more than a hundred flying in a line like that. But now they eat fish loaded with DDT, and so they lay eggs with shells that are too thin. Often the eggs are broken in the nest before the young can hatch."

Yes, I thought, like dinosaurs. If there had been human eyes to see, the last of those doomed creatures, lumbering toward a water hole, would have looked equally sad. I said, "Well, at least we still have shells."

Not answering, he dropped the shell back into his pocket.

"Do you have a large shell collection?"

"Not very. Unless you find them, they're expensive."

"My grandfather made a shell collection."

"I know."

"I'm supposed to catalogue all his collections, and I know nothing about shells. Could you help me?"

"I'm pretty busy."

I said, really annoyed now, "It's my aunt who wants the collection catalogued. And she told me you would help me."

A flush appeared under his deep tan. "All right. When?"

"Shall we say tomorrow at three?"

He turned away without saying good-by. I watched him climb the steps.

For perhaps another five minutes I stayed on the beach, looking out over the water. Against all logic, I felt sorry for Harley Clayton, and regretful that, by relaying the orders of the rich woman he had married, I had brought that flush to his face.

At last I returned to the house and set grimly to

work on the china and crystal. I found listing the glassware easy, because all of it, except for a pair of blue candlesticks—probably Venetian, although I wasn't absolutely sure—was Waterford crystal. I finished a little after six, went to my room, and waited until the dinner gong sounded through the house.

Less than a minute after I entered the dining room, Lisa came in, still wearing her brief white shorts. "Hi, high pockets," Kevin greeted her, and Amy Warren said, "Why, hello, stranger!"

Amy turned to me. "Lisa doesn't join us very often. She likes Galton Beach hamburgers and milk shakes for dinner."

Lisa sat down in the chair Dr. Satherly had occupied the night before. "Not always," she said coolly. She shook out her napkin and laid it across her bare thighs. Would she have come dressed like that to dinner, I wondered, if my aunt had been present at the table?

Mrs. Warren brightened our meal with a chapter-by-chapter account of a biography of the late—or rather, "translated"—Krishnamurti. Perhaps because I had objected to his baiting remarks of the night before, Kevin made none tonight. He just looked bored. So did Lisa. I began to suspect that it was because of Amy's monologues, rather than a preference for hamburgers, that Lisa had appeared so infrequently at the dimmer table. As for her presence tonight, I was almost sure my own presence was responsible. She still did not trust me, and wanted to give me as few chances as possible to work my wiles on Kevin.

When we had finished coffee, Amy went into the library to consult William James again. Lisa moved with Kevin and me out into the hall. She walked toward the

front door, stopped, and turned to look at Kevin, standing beside me at the foot of the stairs.

"Well, aren't you coming?"

"Where?"

"We were going to Galton Beach tonight, remember?"

"Oh, sure." He took a ring of car keys from a pocket.
"Go get the crate. I'll meet you out front."

He tossed the keys. She caught them expertly in one
hand, stood frowning for a moment, and then went out
through the front door, closing it none too gently.

Standing on the second step, I looked down at Kevin.
"In case you haven't noticed, that's a very beautiful
girl. How long do you think you can treat her like that
before she turns to someone else?"

"What gives you the idea I care where she turns?
She's a good-looking kid all right, but that's just it.
She's only eighteen. I prefer my women like you, more
—seasoned."

"You make me sound like an over-the-hill roller
derby racer."

"I thought you'd like that. But about Lisa. She's not
only a kid. She's sort of a weird kid. She was in a car accident. I remember hearing about it just before I went
to Vietnam, so she must have been about twelve then. I
gather that ever since she's been a little peculiar."

"You mean it affected her mentally? She seems bright
enough."

"Oh, there's nothing wrong with her I.Q. But if
you've got any valuables with you, better hide them."

"You mean she steals?" He nodded. "Did she take a
bracelet of Aunt Evelyn's?"

"That's right. Last March, I think it was."

Last March. And yet that same month, Aunt Evelyn had married Lisa's brother.

"See you," he said, and took a limping step toward the door.

"Kevin."

He turned around. "Yes?"

I hesitated, regretting the impulse that had made me call after him. Nevertheless, I said, "Your limp. You did get it in combat, didn't you?"

A horn honked outside. He said, smiling, "Amy been talking to you?"

"Yes. She said you'd been in a brawl in some Saigon bar."

"They don't hand out Purple Hearts for private fights, not even in a fouled-up war like that one. If you like, I'll show you my Purple Heart."

Did he really have such a decoration? Whether he did or did not, he must know I wouldn't demand to see it.

"Sorry," I said, "but I had to ask."

The horn honked again, three long, angry blasts.

"Don't be sorry. How can you and I have that really meaningful relationship I have in mind if we're not frank with each other?"

I laughed. He said, through another prolonged blast of the horn, "So long," and again turned toward the door.

Ten

I went upstairs, knocked on Aunt Evelyn's door, and, when she answered, opened it. A folding tray spanned her lap. "I haven't finished dinner," she said. "Come back in half an hour."

I looked at her plate. String beans, half a baked potato with sour cream and chives, and the remains of a filet mignon. We'd had roast chicken for dinner. Evidently my aunt, not fancying chicken, had told Mrs. Escobar to take it back and bring her a steak. "All right."

In my room almost half an hour later, while I sat repairing chipped nail polish, I heard an MG drive around the corner of the house toward the garage. Why had they come back so soon? A fight? Remembering those angry blasts of the horn, I thought it more than likely. I recapped the bottle of nail polish, set it on my dressing table, and walked down the hall to Aunt Evelyn's room.

Her dinner tray was gone. "Sit down," she said. Then, when I was seated in the straight chair beside her bed: "How did the cataloguing go?"

"All right. I've finished the crystal and china."

"Good. There's silver in the dining room sideboard. Ask Mrs. Escobar for the key. The keys to the collection cases are over there in the top drawer of the highboy. Take them before you leave."

"All right."

Smiling, she studied my face. "Sullen tonight, aren't we? Have you been hearing things about me from Mrs. Escobar, perhaps?"

"No."

"I think you have. Oh, don't worry. I won't fire her. She's far too valuable to me. As for Lorena's child, I did both her and the child a favor. Lorena's mother may die soon. Could a girl like Lorena raise a child herself?"

"Is that why you got Dr. Satherly to trick her into signing those adoption papers?"

"No. I did it for my own convenience. I wanted to keep Lorena here. And I didn't want her sneaking off all the time to visit the child, or pestering me to let her keep him here. The fact remains that all three of those women, and the child, too, are better off than they would have been if a sentimentalist like you had handled the situation.

"And so you might as well drop that air of moral superiority," she went on. "It doesn't impress me. I freely admit that I'm a woman who knows what she wants, and usually gets it. But I pay well for it. I raised Mrs. Escobar's and Lorena's wages fifty percent after Lorena came back from the hospital. Did Mrs. Escobar tell you that?"

I could not keep the scorn out of my voice. "No."

"And Kevin gets a very good salary indeed. Come to

83

think of it, I'm paying you very well."

"How about your husband? Do you pay him well?"

I saw anger in the dark eyes, but she still smiled. "We are all fired up, aren't we? Harley is another matter. But if you think he may inherit my estate, stop worrying. As a matter of fact, I called you in here tonight to show you my will. It's in the wall safe. Take down that picture over there."

I rose and walked over to the picture she indicated, a still life of a jade figurine and a blue luster vase filled with white roses. I took it down, revealing the steel door and dial of a small safe. When I had set the picture on the floor, propped against the wall, I turned back to my aunt. "What's the combination?"

"Take out the drawer of that table over there. The combination is pasted to the bottom."

I walked over to the small rosewood table, set near the long windows that opened onto the balcony. It was charming—early eighteenth-century French, with graceful cabriole legs and a top inlaid with some lighter wood, probably pecan. I switched on the small, crystal-shaded lamp that stood on the table, took out the empty drawer, and turned it upside-down. As I stood there memorizing the series of typed numbers pasted to the drawer's underside, I was aware of my dim reflection in the window glass and, beyond it, the branch of the live oak reaching toward the balcony rail.

I replaced the drawer, walked over to the safe, spun the dial. When I heard a click, I pulled the door open. I saw a small jewel chest of dark blue velvet. No doubt it contained, among other things, the bracelet Amy Warren had helped my aunt recover. Otherwise the safe was empty except for a white, business-sized envelope. On it my aunt had written in her tall backhand, "Last Will and Testament."

When I had carried the envelope over to the bed, my aunt said, "Read it."

Still standing, I unfolded the single sheet of paper. The will, handwritten, was addressed to "Whom it may concern." The first paragraph left five thousand dollars "to my husband, Harley Clayton, provided he is still my husband at the time of my death."

The remaining paragraph read: "All the rest of my estate, both real and personal, I leave to my sister, Madge Dunway Langley. In the event Madge Dunway Langley predeceases me, her share of my estate is to go to her daughter, Jennifer Langley."

The date on the will was less than two weeks old.

I refolded the paper and thrust it into the envelope. "Short but sweet," my aunt said. "And a holograph will, the best kind. It requires no witnesses, and no pettifogging lawyer to draw it up."

"Does Harley know he gets only five thousand dollars?"

"No. Put the envelope back."

I walked across the room and laid the envelope in the safe beside the jewel box.

A muffled crash, somewhere behind me. I spun around.

My aunt's voice was sharp. "Go out on the balcony. See what that is." Then, as I started across the room: "No! Close the safe first."

I went back, closed the safe, spun the dial. Then I crossed to one of the long windows, opened it, and stepped from the air-conditioned room into the humid, overcast night. Refracted light from the window

85

showed me the white wicker armchair, about five feet
to my right, and beside it the wicker table, overturned.
On the balcony floor lay what looked like fragments of
a blue pottery ashtray. I righted the table, and then
stood looking along the balcony.

No light spilled from the windows of the next room,
Amy's. Was she asleep, or still down in the library? Or
was she standing tense in her darkened room, ready to
answer with feigned drowsiness if someone knocked?

Rectangles of light fell from two more rooms along
the balcony. The nearest one, I knew, was Lisa's, and
the other Kevin's. Then I thought of the stairs slanting
down from the balcony. It need not have been Amy or
Kevin or Lisa who had blundered into that table. Harley Clayton could have been up here, or Mrs. Escobar
or her niece, or even someone who was not a member
of the household.

A scrambling sound in the lower branches of the live
oak. With a nervous start, I turned and looked over the
balcony rail. After a moment I saw a white cat, ghostlike in the dark, descending the trunk, head first and
with cautious deliberation. When he was about four
feet from the ground, he completed his descent in one
leap and scampered toward the garage. He was a big
cat. If he had launched himself toward the overhanging
branch from that light table, he easily might have overturned it.

I stepped back into the room's coolness and closed
the door. "It was a cat, I think. He upset that table and
broke an ashtray."

"A big cat? White?" When I nodded, my aunt relaxed visibly. "I don't know how that cat got on the island, but he's always climbing that oak and then jump-

ing onto the balcony. I've given orders that he's to be gotten rid of, but he's still prowling around. Damn! I'm out of cigarettes again."

I brought her a pack from the highboy, and held the lighter for her. The cigarette trembled between her fingers. Evidently she was aware that I had noticed, because after her first drag on the cigarette she said, "Damn that cat. My nerves are pretty bad tonight. I didn't sleep too well last night."

Bad dreams, about a shadowy figure she might or might not have glimpsed in the upstairs hall? And then I thought of that flesh-and-blood invader, the one I had seen the night before. "Did Kevin tell you I saw a trespasser last night?"

"Where?" Her voice was sharp. "What did he look like?"

As I described him, she visibly relaxed. I concluded, "Kevin says he sounds like one of those Cubans who are into gambling and so on in Miami."

"I wouldn't wonder." She seemed irritated rather than alarmed. "I wouldn't wonder at anyone turning up here. When I was a girl, that fence on the landward side was enough to keep people off. But these days!"

Her tone became brooding. "Sometimes I think I'll just give up, sell the island, and buy a house in Boca Raton. But I hate the thought."

Yes, it would be hard for anyone, living or dead, to make her surrender her small kingdom. I said, "Don't you think you should at least keep those balcony doors locked?"

"What good would that do? Anyone who wanted to could just break the glass. But it would be a very stupid thief who would invade a house with six people in it—

87

seven, counting you. And I can always phone the gate-house, or phone the sheriff in Galton Beach and have a patrol car blocking the other end of the causeway."

After a moment I said, "But your bracelet—"

"That was not a professional thief," she said coldly. "That was a member of this household. And the thief knows now that a second try would be very unwise indeed."

She paused. Was she expecting me to ask the identity of the "member of the household"? When I remained silent, she said, "Anyway, professional thieves avoid islands. There aren't enough escape routes. No, trespassers don't frighten me. They just annoy me. That's why I got the Dobermans.

"I'm tired now," she added. "Take those keys to the collection cases before you go."

I went over to the highboy and opened the top drawer. "They're in the brown envelope," she said. "Be sure to bring them back when you're finished with them."

"All right." I took out a manila envelope, hearing a metallic jingle inside it, and closed the drawer. "Well, good night."

I went out into the hall and walked down it to my room.

Only minutes later I was out in the hall again, hand still on the knob of the door I had slammed behind me, throat still rigid from the half-strangled scream that had burst from it.

A door on the opposite side of the hall opened and Kevin, still in the tan chinos and brown shirt he had worn earlier that evening, limped rapidly toward me. I relinquished the knob and leaned against the wall, with my stomach tightened into a queasy knot.

"Under my dressing table," I managed to say. "A tarantula."

Without answering, he went into my room and closed the door. I still leaned against the wall, hoping I would not be sick. After a moment I heard something strike the floor. The flat-heeled sandal I'd taken off? One of his own shoes? Two more stout thwacks were followed by an interval of silence. Then he opened the door. In one hand he held a wad of my white facial tissues. "Got him. Want to view the remains?"

"No!" I shuddered. "It was in my bedroom slipper."

When I entered my room a few minutes earlier, I had decided that, since I felt wakeful, I might as well wash out some underthings and the drip-dry blouse and skirt I had worn on my journey down from New York. I stripped off my dress and replaced it with a robe. Then, sitting on the edge of the bed, I took off my sandals and reached down for one of my pink bedroom slippers, which really weren't slippers, but felt-soled, ankle-high boots of lightweight cloth.

Something in the toe of the boot moved. I could feel the movement and see the shifting, lumpish shape of it under the pink cloth. I flung the boot from me, and it landed on its side on the floor. A black, hairy spider, as large as a silver dollar, scuttled over the braided rug, over a stretch of bare floor, and disappeared under the dressing table. It was then that I gave a strangled scream and ran out into the hall.

"They hang out in the stable," Kevin said. "We kept them pretty well cleaned out until your aunt sold that mare, but I guess now they're coming back in."

I looked again at the wadded tissue in his hand, and

then away. "But how did it get up here, in my slipper?"

He shrugged. "How do the filthy things get anyplace? But it wouldn't have killed you, even if it had bitten you. It would just have made you pretty sick for a few days. Its poison can kill insects, and even birds, but not humans." He paused. "You okay now?"

"Yes."

"Then I'll get rid of this thing." He limped toward his door and then stopped to look back at me, grinning. "Better inspect your bed before you snuggle between the sheets."

Maybe Kevin had only been indulging his sometimes peculiar sense of humor. But as soon as I went back into my room, I did strip off the chintz coverlet, then the two light blankets, and the top sheet. Nothing.

For a few moments I stood motionless, thinking. Had that repulsive thing, unaided, made its way from the stable at the rear of the clearing into the house, up to the second floor, and into this room overlooking the front lawn?

I imagined someone earlier tonight, or even last night, back there behind the closed stable door. Someone with a wide-mouthed jar in hand who had turned on the light, and then stalked the hideous, scurrying creatures.

But why? Out of sheer malice? Or a desire to frighten me enough that I'd pack my bag?

I thought of Lisa, whose jealousy, however unjustified, might give her reason to want to speed me on my way. I thought of Amy, who might fear that her benefactor's doubts of her powers might be reinforced by the presence of a skeptical niece. I thought of Kevin, whose parting injunction to search my bed certainly had not been intended to settle my nerves. Kevin, who in his Saigon days might well have been involved in some episode he wanted to hide. Had he, despite his offhand air, been irritated or even alarmed by my question about his limp?

And then there was Harley Clayton who, except for those few moments when we talked of the seashell he'd found, and of that line of pelicans flying past, had looked at me with a go-to-hell expression in his eyes.

Beneath my lingering fright and revulsion, anger began to stir. Probably no one had dumped that thing into my slipper. But if someone had—well, this was my grandfather's house, and my mother's, and my own legacy. It would take more than a spider to make me leave it before I was ready.

I went into the bathroom and turned on the water in the basin. Not taking any chances, I upended the small wicker hamper. Skirt, blouse, pantyhose, and a bra spilled out onto the tiled floor, but nothing else.

Grimly, I began to do my washing.

Eleven

Again I had trouble getting to sleep, and so did not leave my room until past nine the next morning. As I descended the spiral stairs, I saw Amy Warren turn away from a mahogany table that stood near the dining room archway. She held at least half a dozen letters in her hand.

She greeted me with a bright smile. "You certainly are a late riser, aren't you? But don't worry. I left some breakfast for you."

"Thanks." I added, "I didn't get to sleep until late."

"I know how it is, in a house you're unaccustomed to."

"It wasn't that. I'd found a tarantula in my room."

She drew a quick breath and shuddered. "What did you do?"

"I ran out of my room. Kevin had heard me scream, and so he went in and killed it." I paused. "Didn't you hear anything?" I had wondered about that. Surely Lisa, and Amy, too, if she were in her room by then, should have heard the slam of my door and then Kevin's voice and mine in the hall. But neither of them had opened her door to investigate.

"No, I didn't hear anything. What time did it happen, dear?"

"Around ten."

"I was still down in the library. Besides, I'm a little deaf, you know."

I hadn't been aware of anything wrong with her hearing. I looked at the sheaf of letters in her hand. "The morning mail?"

"Yes. Harley went to the post office early today."

"I don't suppose there's anything for me." Still, if my mother had written the day I left New York, the letter might be here by now.

"No. Except for one letter for your aunt, they're all mine."

"Are you sure?" I was looking more closely now at the topmost of the envelopes in her hand. Her thumb obscured part of the address. But I could see the word "Miss" written in a small hand that was not my mother's, and the final three letters of the surname, "—ley."

She brought the envelopes close to her face, and then gave a dismayed little squeal. "This one's yours!" She handed it to me. "I guess I simply must get new glasses."

If she had misread Langley as Warren, she certainly did need new glasses. She leafed rapidly through the remaining envelopes. "Yes, except for Evelyn's, these all seem to be mine. But perhaps you'd better—" She held the sheaf out to me.

"No, I'm sure they're yours. Well, I think I'll get breakfast."

93

As I walked into the empty dining room, I reflected that perhaps I had discovered one way Amy Warren gathered information. At some time during Amy's stay here, had some old army pal written to Kevin? "How's the gimpy leg?" he might have written. "I'll never forget that night in the Lotus Bar, and I'll bet you won't either, even stoned as you were. What was the name of the guy who shot you, that PFC from Oklahoma?"

Yes, a friend might well have written a letter saying something like that. And it might well have ended up torn into scraps and flushed away in the bathroom that connected Amy's room with my aunt's.

When I had served myself eggs and toast, I opened my letter. It was a short note from the girl who had moved into my apartment for a month.

> I've been here only a few hours, but I can't resist telling you that your apartment is sheer heaven. No roommates trying to borrow this or that, no line of someone else's pantyhose dangling from the shower curtain rod. I don't know how I'll ever express my gratitude. Maybe I'll stock your fridge with enough sauce that you can throw another of your wonderful cocktail brawls, this time for about forty people.
>
> Love and gratitude,
Jonesy.

That last sentence was sheer fantasy. Jonesy has one of those New York glamor jobs—stenographer in the office of an independent film producer—which pay almost nothing. To buy even one bottle of "sauce," she would have to eat hot dogs for lunch three days in a row. Besides, my apartment would not hold forty people, even if they stood in the bathtub and hung from the window ledge. The largest party I had ever given there was a sedate four-to-six gathering for my boss, Jonesy, and a half-dozen other people. But Amy Warren no doubt would have been titillated by the thought of me as a thrower of large, extravagant, and drunken parties. Feeling mingled amusement and annoyance, I folded Jonesy's letter and put it in the pocket of my denim skirt.

After breakfast I went to Mrs. Escobar, obtained the keys to the huge old mahogany buffet in the dining room, and spent the rest of the morning and the early afternoon cataloguing just about every imaginable product of the silversmith's art, from a George Second epergne to a pair of sterling poultry shears from the old Baltimore firm of Samuel Kirk.

A few minutes before three, though, I was in the library, uncomfortably but helplessly aware that my pulses had stepped up their beat. I had unlocked one of the étagères, and stood looking at the rainbow-hued array of shells, when Harley walked into the room to stand beside me.

"Hello," I said, "and thanks for coming."

He acknowledged that with an unsmiling nod and then said, "The best way would be to take the shelves out of the cabinet, one by one."

"All right. I found a square of felt in the buffet. We'll put the shells on that as we catalogue them."

We sat down at the library table, he with one of the glass shelves before him, I with my open ledger. His big fingers almost reverentially careful, he picked up a cone-shaped shell, rosy-brown in color, and about five inches long.

"Glory-of-the-Sea," he said, "or *conus glorianaris.* This specimen probably came from the Philippines or the Solomon Islands. Anyway, from somewhere in the southwest Pacific."

He spelled out the Latin name for me. I wrote it down and then asked, "Approximate value?"

"It would bring at least a thousand at auction."

"You're kidding."

"No. There are only about seventy specimens extant, and most of them are in museums."

He laid Glory-of-the-Sea on the length of felt. For a moment his hand hovered over the glass tray. Then he picked up a large fluted shell. Its color, white with just the faintest tinge of blue, reminded me of fine porcelain. "This is a sea snail," he said, *"murex alabaster.* To me it's the most beautiful of all shells, even though it isn't particularly rare."

"With those fluted spines along the back it looks like a tropical fish."

He nodded. "Back in the days of Nineveh and Tyre people thought so, too. In fact, *murex* means 'purple fish.' "

"But it's not purple!"

"No, but three thousand years ago people around the Mediterranean made a dye by extracting a yellowish fluid from sea snails and then boiling it. The end product was purple—royal Tyrian purple."

The cataloguing went slowly. Each shell that he picked up provoked questions from me and answers from him. He seemed a different man now. Dark blue eyes animated, he showed me a carrier shell, so heavily camouflaged with dead shells, pebbles, and bits of coral it had attached to itself that you could scarcely see the carrier. He named for me several species of cowries, and told me how ancient peoples all over the world had used cowries as money. In fact, he said, the image of that shell as money was so strong in the ancient world that the first coin minted by the Greeks in Lydia about 750 B.C. was in the shape of a cowry.

Something in his own words must have brought a troubling thought to mind, because he fell suddenly silent. I looked at him sitting there, turning the cowry over and over in his hand, and with that closed look beginning to settle over his face again. And because I didn't like that look, I burst out recklessly, "Why did you ever come here?"

He looked at me for a silent few seconds, his eyes acknowledging that he knew what I had meant. Why had he ever come to this island owned by that rich woman upstairs, and why was he still here?

Finally he said, "I'm like almost everyone else. I have a hostage to fortune."

I said, after a moment, "Your sister?"

"Yes. Until she was almost twelve, she was the nicest, sunniest, most uncomplicated kid you could imagine. I changed all that."

"How on earth could you have—"

"Oh, I did, all right. I didn't mean to. It was an accident, but an accident that wouldn't have happened if I'd had better control of my temper."

He told me then that he had come home for spring vacation from the University of Florida, that April seven years before. His first day home he phoned a local girl to whom he had given his fraternity pin—"Good Lord, I can't even remember her name now!"—only to learn that she was sending the pin back. She had become engaged to a dentist fifteen years her senior.

"It seems silly now, but I was sore as hell. I went out to the garage, intending to drive around for an hour or so until I cooled off. Lisa followed me out there. Some other little girl had invited her for lunch, and she wanted me to drop her off. At first I said no, but she looked as if she were about to cry, so I told her to get in."

Eager to be rid of the child so that he could be alone with his hurt and anger, he had driven too fast. At an intersection he risked running through a light that had just turned red. Another car slammed into his.

"I was only shaken up, but Lisa was thrown out of the car. Not through the windshield, thank God. But the door on her side flew open, and she hit the pavement."

Even though her injuries had included concussion, there was no brain damage. "None that the doctors could find, anyway. Maybe it was just the shock of the accident that did it. Or maybe—just maybe—it was a personality change that would have taken place even without the accident. But anyway, she became a different child. Even when she had recovered completely, she was still whiny and demanding. And the next year she was expelled from school. The principal said that she had become unmanageable, cutting classes and defying her teachers."

Was her expulsion just for truancy and impudence, I wondered, or had she begun to steal from her classmates?

"Dad put her in private school. Soon after that I went through flight training and was sent to Vietnam.

When Dad died, I came home on leave, settled Lisa with this cousin of my father's, and went back to Vietnam. From Cousin Helen's letters I knew that Lisa was giving her trouble, but it wasn't until I was discharged nearly a year ago that I found out how bad things were. Lisa had been expelled from two more schools, and her behavior at the last one had landed her in juvenile court. Cousin Helen's fairly well off, so she arranged with the judge that sentence would be suspended if Lisa went to this special school for a year. It calls itself the Winton School for Girls, but it's really kind of a posh reform school and psychiatric sanitarium combined."

He paused for a moment, fingering the shell in his hand. Then he went on, "She was seventeen by the time I got home, and out of the Winton School, and running around with a pretty sick crowd. Oh, she wasn't into drugs or booze. She likes her swimming and tennis too much to mess up that way. But some of her friends were into drugs, so I was afraid it was only a matter of time. I didn't know what the hell to do, especially since I had problems of my own."

He stopped speaking. After a moment I asked cautiously, "What problems?"

He shrugged. "I don't want to rehash the damn war. Let's just say I didn't enjoy it." He looked down at the shell in his hand, and I wondered what else he was seeing. Smoke and flame boiling up from what only seconds before had been a village? "I knew I could probably get a job with a commercial airline, but I didn't even want to fly again, at least not right away."

And then one day he had received a phone call from his father's old friend, Evelyn Dunway. "I told her a little of my problems, and she asked me over for a drink. After we'd talked for half an hour or so, she suggested that I ought to take some sort of manual job for a while. I'd been thinking the same thing. Then she offered me the caretaker's job here. Lisa could come to the island, too, she said."

"Did Lisa like the idea?"

"Very much. She'd loved the island the few times she'd visited it as a child. And I knew that she was worried about the kids she was going around with. Even though she kept telling me to shut up about it, I could tell she was afraid she'd get mixed up in something that would land her in jail or a psychiatric ward."

"And so the two of you came here."

"Yes." He placed the shell back on the length of felt.

Perhaps he wanted me to ask the other and more important questions that hovered between us. But I couldn't, not then. I was afraid that he would look at me with suddenly cold eyes and say, "That's a strictly personal matter."

He glanced at the watch strapped to his big wrist. "Almost five. I'll have to get down to the causeway. There's a chuckhole I want to fill in before dark."

He looked at the étagère, and then at me. "Three more shelves to go. We didn't get very far with the cataloguing, did we?"

"No." His faint smile, and the one curving my own lips, acknowledged that we had dawdled deliberately. Well, I would make up for it by working twice as hard on the other inventories—after we had finished with the seashells.

He began to lift the shells from the felt onto the

glass. "Tomorrow at the same time?"

"Yes," I said.

Dinner that night was a rather strained affair. Lisa was present, but not speaking to Kevin. He tried various overtures, which ranged from the flattering to the mildly insulting. After receiving nothing for his pains but a stony stare from Lisa's beautiful gray eyes, he grinned at me and shrugged. From then on he paid elaborate attention to Amy Warren, who tonight had chosen for her subject matter, not a topic from the field of the occult, but a eulogy of the late Mr. Warren, "who had been worth any six of the sort of young men you see around nowadays."

After dinner I joined Amy in the library long enough to select a book. Evidently Aunt Evelyn had bought no books since falling heir to the house. The most recent novel on the shelves was *Gone with the Wind.* I considered rereading that, but finally decided upon renewing my old acquaintance with Jane Austen's *Emma.* I took it upstairs with me and read several chapters of Emma's adventures with Mr. Knightly. Then, feeling restless, I wandered over to a window and looked down at the east lawn.

An almost full moon tonight, shining down on the grass and on a group of hibiscus bushes set in a circular bed, their scarlet blossoms looking black under the flood of blue-white radiance. I thought of how beautiful the beach and sea must be. No, better not walk over there alone.

But at least I could go down to the lawn. I left my room, descended the stairs, and stepped out onto the porch. I had started down the steps when I saw a man moving across the grass toward me, blond hair gleaming in the moonlight. He stopped at the foot of the steps.

"I was going to leave a note for you on the hall table. I've found two more bad places on the causeway. Is it all right if we start work on the shells at two tomorrow? Then I can work on the causeway from four on, and maybe finish by dark."

"Two will be fine." He did not turn away, and so I said, "It's such a gorgeous night that I couldn't stay in the house."

"Are you going down to the beach?"

"No. I'd just as soon not run into any more strangers."

For a moment I had the distinct impression that he wanted to accompany me. But if so, he must have thought better of it, because he said, "If you want to walk down to the beach, you'll be perfectly safe."

"You mean, because you put barbed wire at the end of that dock?"

"Partly that. About the only way someone could get onto the island now would be to use wire cutters, or swim." He hesitated, and then went on, "So if you do see someone you don't know, he won't be a trespasser."

I said, puzzled, "You mean he'll be someone you've allowed on the island?"

"No, I have nothing to do with it." His voice was emphatic. "And I'm telling you this only so that you won't be frightened again."

"You mean friends of Kevin's sometimes—"

"Look, Jennifer." It was the first time he had used my name. "This is Kevin's business. He's told me about it, and I neither approve nor disapprove. All you need to know is that it's safe for you to walk around anytime you please."

I said slowly, "If Kevin's mixed up with the sort of man I saw the other night—"

"Kevin says he didn't recognize the description you gave. Sure, Kevin could be lying, but even if he is— well, maybe your impression of the man wasn't accurate."

"But he was only a few feet away! And he'd lit this lighter—"

"You saw a man with a scar on his face. A man can acquire a scar in any number of ways, you know. If you don't believe me, visit a veterans' hospital sometime. Maybe it was just that you were upset and frightened, running into a strange man that far from the house. Besides, a facial scar is a kind of visual cliché. How many dozens of TV and movie gangsters have you seen with scarred cheeks?"

I stood silent, remembering the aura of evil that had seemed to emanate from that sharp face bent above the lighter flame. But perhaps that impression had been due more to my imagination than to any quality of the man himself. And Harley was right about all those scarred hoodlums on TV.

He said, "You can mention this conversation to your aunt if you want to. But you might be getting Kevin into trouble. It would be different if he were putting her in any danger, but he isn't. Any risks he is running are strictly his own."

"No, I won't tell her." My aunt, I had begun to suspect, could give any common or garden variety of blackmailer a few lessons in using information to one's own advantage and the profound disadvantage of others. And when it came down to it, I liked Kevin a lot better than my aunt. I added, "But I do wish you would tell me—"

"No." His voice was positive. "I'm not going to tell you about it. And I doubt if you'll get any information out of Kevin."

No, Kevin would tell me no more than he chose to. And by questioning him I might make trouble between him and Harley. My impression was that the relations between the two men, while not close, were amicable enough, and I did not want to change that. "I won't mention this to Kevin."

"All right. See you tomorrow."

I went up to my room and exchanged my sandals for sneakers. Feeling a little foolish, I again put the can of hair spray in my shoulder bag before leaving the house.

Tonight the flooding moonlight, refracted by the white gravel on the wide path, was so brilliant that I could have read fairly small print by it. I paused at the intersecting path and looked for a few moments at the pavilion. In this blue-white light, its concrete resembled marble. You could almost imagine that once it had stood, a temple to some Grecian god, in an olive grove near Athens. I walked on, and then stopped at the top of the limestone steps leading down to the beach.

Kevin stood down there on the sand, back turned to me. In that brilliant light his thin figure and curly dark head were unmistakable. He carried something draped over his arm. I was about to call down to him when my eye was caught by the white cap of a swimmer moving toward shore.

In another few seconds I saw it was Lisa. She stood up and removed her cap, releasing that mass of pale hair. Then she waded ashore, naked as the Venus de Milo, but not as coy. In fact, not coy at all. She strolled up onto the sand and put on the robe Kevin held for her. Then, arms around each other's waists, and her head on a level with his, they walked away down the beach.

I stood there, feeling a little miffed, but glad that I had given no serious attention to Kevin's verbal passes at me. For a while longer I looked out over the sea, sparkling under a moon-washed sky that was only a few shades darker than its daytime blue. Then I walked back to the house.

Twelve

The cataloguing of my grandfather's shells proceeded no faster the next afternoon. Nor could our slow pace be blamed on Amy Warren's interruptions, even though she did tiptoe into the library twice and, with an elaborate air of *not* interrupting, took down a book from the shelves and tiptoed out. No, it was just that each shell provided so much matter for conversation. Harley gave me not only the scientific name, approximate price, and probable geographical origin of each, but also other information concerning it. For instance, he told me that the scallop shell had been a favorite decorative motif for hundreds of years, turning up in about everything from Edward the Third's design for the Order of the Garter to Botticelli's "Birth of Venus."

And we exchanged information that had nothing to do with shells. I learned that he liked classical music, New Orlenas jazz, and some but not all rock, and that his favorite modern novel was *Catch 22*. I told him that I sometimes loathed New York, but needed only to look at the Plaza Hotel fountain, or walk down Fifty-seventh Street past the art galleries and antique stores to fall in love with the town all over again.

Neither of us mentioned my aunt, or his sister, or Kevin. I think we both wanted to forget for a while that anything existed outside that room, and ourselves, and the bright array of shells on the table between us.

At last he said, looking at the still-untouched shelves of the étagère, "There seems to be plenty of work left for tomorrow."

I said, with constraint, "Yes, there does, doesn't there?"

"Well, I'll see you then."

Amy Warren was absent from the dinner table that night. By means of Lorena's few words of English, and my dimly remembered Spanish, I gathered that Mrs. Warren had a headache. Lisa, too, was absent. Apparently she had felt it safe to indulge in Galton Beach hamburgers and a milk shake.

With only two of us at the table, Kevin plied me with compliments and with thinly veiled invitations to what the French call the dance of love. At last I said, "Knock it off already."

His forehead wrinkled quizzically. "I was standing at the head of the beach stairs last night," I explained, "when Lisa came out of the water. I'd say you have enough to manage as it is."

His smile was only a little abashed. "Can I help it if I have Turkish blood?"

"Perhaps not, my passionate pasha, but I can keep from paying it any mind."

"Okay, okay. From now on we're just good friends."

I looked at the attractive, teasing face under the tumbled dark hair. What was Kevin like, really? And what was he up to? Dealing marijuana to associates who sold it on the mainland? Perhaps. That was probably something that Harley would disapprove of mildly, but not enough so as to blow the whistle on Kevin. I hoped it was not marijuana, not when such transactions were still a felony.

Kevin asked, with an innocent air, "How is the shell inventory progressing? Briskly, I trust."

"Briskly enough." To divert him from that subject, I said, "I've been thinking about that tarantula. Do you think Lisa could have put it in my slipper?"

"Same thought occurred to me. I asked her, and she denied it. But she could have been capable of it. You've had her pretty worried, you know, and as I told you, she can be a weird girl."

More than a weird girl, I thought, remembering my conversation with Harley the day before. A deeply troubling girl, both to herself and to the brother who blamed himself for her behavior.

"Of course," Kevin went on, "she'd never have gotten so up tight if she'd known you were frigid—okay, okay!" He raised his hands in mock surrender. "You don't have to throw anything. Besides," he added, looking over my shoulder, "here comes our dessert."

After dinner I started to my room and then, in the upstairs hall, hesitated beside the telephone. By this time I had expected to have at least a note from my mother, but none had arrived. I picked up the phone and asked to reverse charges to my mother's number.

I heard her say, "Yes, operator, I'll accept the charges," and then: "Oh, darling. I was just about to write to you."

There had been tension in her voice. "Is anything wrong?"

"Well, yes, dear. Do you remember how Beulah had accepted all those stories of mine?"

"Yes." Beulah, that bottomless fount of far-out titles.

"She was going to publish three of them in her October issues, and five more later on. I was counting on the money."

I said indignantly, "You mean she's gone back on—"

"Oh, no! It's not her fault. The publisher has folded all her magazines. She's out of a job, and I've got eight manuscripts on my hands."

"Mother, I'm sorry, but you can send them out to other—"

"There's not much point in that. Beulah always insisted upon such a different slant. Other editors won't want them, not without a lot of revision. And there are all these bills to pay—"

"Mother, don't panic." I thought rapidly. Despite my earnings at the Unicorn Shop, I was not especially solvent. During the past eight months, I'd been making payments on the VW and on furniture for my apartment. Still . . . "I can send you a check for two hundred. I'll have plenty to get home on after Aunt Evelyn pays me. And I have around another six hundred in savings. If you'll phone the bank and ask them to send me a withdrawal slip—"

"I am not so old," she said with dignity, "that I have to turn to my child for support."

"Oh, Mother! It's only a loan."

"No, dear. Since I've felt too unstrung to even start those revisions right now, I've accepted a position."

"What sort of position?"

"You know Jimmy's Tavern?"

My heart sank. I did know Jimmy's Tavern, a few miles outside of that Hudson River town. It had third-rate rock and country musicians, a juke box that blared whenever the entertainers took a break, noisy customers who ranged in age from late adolescence to early senility, and frequent fist fights, some so prolonged and violent that state police cars came screaming onto the graveled parking lot. Jimmy himself—Jimmy Brockman—was a stout man of fity-odd, with a bald head and a look of jovial insincerity.

I said, "What about Jimmy's Tavern?"

"Well, I think I told you that Mr. Brockman came up to me in the supermarket one day a few months ago and said he remembered me from the days when I was with Bud Easterly's Orchestra, and that if I ever wanted to sing at his place—"

"Mother! Surely you haven't—"

"But I have. I called him yesterday. I start next week. He'll pay fifteen dollars a night, plus my share of what—whatever—"

"Whatever the customers toss into the kitty?"

"Yes. I know it sounds undignified. But it's only until I can pay these bills, Jenny, and then get back to writing. And it will be like the old days, singing again."

It would not be like the old days, when her admirers, as young as, or younger than herself, gathered below the bandstand. There would be no twenty-piece orchestra backing her up. Probably there would be just a pianist, a guitarist, and drummer, none of whom had even been alive when Bud Easterly was popular, and to all of whom the verb "to swing" meant something quite different than it had to those crew-cut young men and dirndl-skirted girls in those long-vanished ballrooms. True, Jimmy's middle-aged customers might like her. But since she was still attractive, some of them might not, as my mother would phrase it, keep their hands to themselves. What seemed to me even worse, somehow, was that Jimmy's young customers might express their disapproval with groans or sarcastically loud applause and whistles.

"Mother, wouldn't you rather come down here?"

"I have not been invited."

"What if I can get Aunt Evelyn to invite you? This singing idea won't work out, Mother. You may end up so upset it will take you a lot longer to get back to writing. Let me deposit that two hundred to your account at your bank. That will cover at least some of the bills, won't it?"

"Yes, but—"

"Then write checks for what you owe, send out those manuscripts, and come down here. You know quite a lot about furniture. You can help me with that when I get to it."

"I'd much rather do that, Jenny." Her voice was so quiet, so wistful, that I realized that she herself had felt misgivings about that singing job. "But probably Evelyn—"

"I'll ask her. I'll ask her right now, and call you back." I hung up, took a deep breath, and walked toward my aunt's room.

When I first knocked, there was no answer. I knocked again. My aunt said in an impatient voice, "Come in."

I opened the door. Whether or not Amy Warren still had her headache, she was in attendance upon my aunt.

Between her straight chair and the bed stood a small table. It held cards, larger than ordinary playing cards, some of them laid out in rows, the others still stacked. Tarot cards, I thought. Those cards, and the annoyed faces of the two women looking at me through the subdued light, gave me an unpleasant sense of having interrupted some ancient secret rite. Again, as when I heard that unintelligible chanting, I felt a cool ripple down my spine. My intelligence told me that Amy Warren was either a fraud, or self-deluded. It was only something atavistic in me, something inherited from my remotest ancestors, that believed and sent that chill down my body.

"Oh, it's you," my aunt said. "I can't see you now." Then, as I started to turn away: "Oh, all right. Tell me about it, whatever it is. Amy, could you come back in about fifteen minutes? No, leave the cards."

"Alrighty," Mrs. Warren said. Eyes curious behind the butterfly glasses, she smiled at me as she passed me in the doorway.

"Close the door, Jennifer, and come over here."

I sat down in the chair Amy had vacated. One of the Tarot cards which had been played out, I noticed, was the Hanged Man. My aunt said, "I realize it's probably all nonsense, but it passes the time."

I made no comment. She said, "Well, what is it, Jennifer?"

"I wondered if you would ask my mother down here." I explained about the eight manuscripts and the job at Jimmy's Tavern.

My aunt said, "Imagine Madge, at her age, wanting to sing in a night club!"

"Many topflight singers are older than Mother. Peggy

Lee, for instance, and Ella Fitzgerald. But that tavern isn't the right place for her. And so, if you'll ask her down here—"

"Sorry. It's out of the question."

"Why? There are plenty of vacant rooms in this house."

"But I don't choose to have her here."

After several seconds I asked, "Why do you hate her?"

"I don't hate her. She just bores and irritates me. She always has, ever since we were both small children. She was always making up to Father, trying to climb into his lap, or running to fetch his paper."

It figured, I thought. Madge Dunway had been number two, and so, like Avis, she had tried harder.

"And later on, when we were both at school in St. Augustine, she was such a bleeding heart. She was always inviting the dopiest girl in her class, someone no one else liked, to stay here for Easter vacation. Once it was a girl who had acne and a stutter."

She was like that now. I thought of my mother on the phone, her gaze going again and again to the interrupted work on her desk, while she listened for half an hour or more to the old lady across the street who called her every morning.

I asked, "And still later?" Better that she get it out of her system before my mother arrived.

"You mean Ray." Her voice was cold. "All right, your father was an attractive man, and at first I was the one who interested him. I didn't like her taking him away, and I still don't know how she did it."

"Were you really in love with him, enough to marry him?"

She looked at the opposite wall. After a while she said, in that cold voice, "Probably not."

For a few seconds, though, her face had been unguarded. I had seen her mouth draw down at the corner, as if tasting some bitterness at the core of her being.

Suddenly, and for the first time, I wondered at the great change which had occurred sometime years ago in my aunt's life. According to my mother, the young Evelyn Dunway had not been popular with her own sex. But she had always been so surrounded by young men that other girls had found it expedient to keep up at least a pretense of friendship with her. She had attended uncounted parties in St. Augustine, and few people had ever declined her invitations to parties here on the island.

But by the time I spent my childhood summer here, she had become a veritable recluse, even though she was only in her early thirties. No one had visited her except her lawyer, Benjamin Clayton, nor could I remember her ever dressing up to go to a party. And during these last few days her only visitor had been her doctor. As far as I knew, she had received no flowers or get-well cards. Except for the garrulous widow she had picked up in a beauty parlor, she seemed quite literally without friends.

What had done that to her? Some event of which I had no knowledge? Or had it been merely Ray Langley's marriage to her sister? Perhaps. Perhaps his defection had been such a blow to her heart, or her swollen pride, or both, that she, on the surface the most un-Victorian of women, had reacted like a jilted maiden of the 1880's. She had secluded herself, not in a cloister, but on this island, among people who were economically dependent upon her, and therefore unable to disregard her wishes or injure her ego without fear of instant reprisal.

The thought made me like her no better. But for the first time I felt a little sorry for her. I said into the silence, "Then you won't ask her down here?"

"I told you I wouldn't."

I sighed. "Then I'd better start packing."

Her voice was sharp. "Why?"

"I'd better get back to New York." Once there I was sure I could persuade Mother to give up that singing job. And with the money I had in savings, we would both make out until the Unicorn Shop opened, and she sold her manuscripts. "Someone else," I said, "can finish the catalogue."

She began angrily, "You know I want that catalogue! And you know I won't have some stranger . . ." Then she broke off and laughed. "You're a lot more like me than you realize, Jennifer. You drive a hard bargain."

"I wasn't trying to bargain."

She shrugged. "Well, anyway, tell her to come. I won't see much of her, as long as I'm shut away up here with this damned leg."

"Thank you." I rose. "I'll call her back."

My mother sounded happy and excited at the news. "I phoned the airline while I was waiting for you to call back. There's a flight that gets into St. Augustine at seven-thirty every night. Suppose I fly down next Sunday. That'll give me several days to get these manuscripts off, along with letters outlining how I could revise them."

"Seven-thirty, Sunday night. I'll meet you."

"And give my love to both Evelyn and Ben."

Ben!

"Mother, Aunt Evelyn didn't marry Ben Clayton. He's been dead for several years."

There was a bewildered silence. "But, Jenny! Her letter—"

"You and I jumped to the wrong conclusion. She married Ben Clayton's son."

"Ben—Clayton's—*son!*" Then after another silent interval, she said in an awed voice, "That Evelyn. She's a law unto herself."

"Yes." And that isn't the worst of it, I wanted to add. The worst is that I've fallen in love with him.

But that was something I hoped my mother would never find out. "See you Sunday," I said. "Good night, Mother."

Thirteen

About nine on Saturday morning, while I moved about the elegant but obviously little-used drawing room across the hall from the dining room, I looked through the window and saw Dr. Satherly's dark red sedan come up the curving drive, followed by a white panel truck with the words "Invalid Supplies" painted in black letters on its side. Two brawny men, clad in hospital whites, emerged from the truck and accompanied the doctor into the house. As I entered Federal mirrors and oil landscapes of the Hudson River School in a ledger, I could hear the distant sound of furniture being moved about on the second floor. After a while the two white-clad men, carrying the hospital bed and the traction equipment, emerged from the house, stowed their burdens in the truck, and drove off. A little later I saw Dr. Satherly leave.

At noon I was summoned to Aunt Evelyn's room, to find her lying on the magnificent four-poster I remembered, a pair of crutches propped against the wall beside her. She handed me a check for a hundred and eighty dollars.

In the library around three that afternoon, Harley restored the last of the shell-laden glass shelves to the étagère. I stood beside him, holding the ledger in which I had entered the scientific and popular names, probable geographical origin, and probable value of more than two hundred specimens.

Harley said, "Well, we've finished."

"Yes."

He didn't move away. We stood there, looking not at each other, but at the shell cabinet.

"There's a shell in the window of the bar in Galton Beach. It's one of the largest conch shells ever found on this coast. Would you like to see it?"

"Yes."

"If you don't mind riding in the pickup truck, we could drive over there around five o'clock, say."

We were looking at each other now. I could tell that he knew, as well as I did, that it would not be a good idea for us to drive to Galton Beach.

"All right," I said. "I'll walk down to the gate at five."

Two hours later we drove over the causeway in the pickup truck. Today the sky was streaked by hazy cirrus clouds. Under the shifting light and shadow, the shallow water looked sometimes blue and sometimes aquamarine or emerald. The clouds, Harley said, were probably outriders of a tropical storm brewing far to the south in the Caribbean. We said almost nothing else to each other until the truck rattled off the causeway.

Just as Galton Beach was a sad little town, the Palmetto was a sad little bar. The line of scarred booths of yellow oak along one wall were empty. The bar that stretched along the other wall also was empty except for an old man who looked broodingly into the depths of a glass beer mug, a young soldier with one chevron who fingered a shot glass and stared blankly at his reflection in the bar mirror, and, at the far end, a furtive-looking middle-aged couple who, turned to face each other on their bar stools, talked in low tones. On the juke box, country singers wailed of freight trucks, endless highways, and wives who might or might not be waiting. A sign above the cash register advised that just as the bank did not serve drinks, the Palmetto did not cash checks.

The proprietor-bartender, a stout, youngish man wearing a long white apron over blue jeans, took the giant conch shell from its nest of faded pink crepe paper in the window. Harley and I looked at the shell. Then we sat down in a booth and ordered draft beer.

A few moments after the proprietor had placed glass mugs on the table and then returned to the bar, Harley said, "I have to talk to you."

I didn't ask what about. I knew.

"About a week after I took the caretaker job, I came into the cottage and found a box from Tiffany's on the table. Inside was a wallet of ostrich leather, with solid gold corners, and stamped with my initials. I took it to her and said thanks, but I didn't want it."

"What did she say?"

"She looked as if she'd like to kill me right there on the spot. Then she laughed and said, 'Don't worry, Joseph. I'm not going to snatch at your cloak.'"

After a moment I said, "Oh, yes. Young Joseph and Potiphar's wife, in the Bible."

"I expected her to fire me, but she didn't, and I was glad. It was good to work alone at simple jobs. What was more important, Lisa seemed perfectly content on the island. I knew that was partly because of Kevin, and I worried about that a little. He's almost eleven years older than she is, and he's a guy who's kind of hard to read. But even so, he was an improvement over the crowd she'd been running with in St. Augustine."

He took a swallow of beer. On the juke box, Johnny Cash and his wife sang of their intention to make their separate ways to Jackson, now that the fire had gone out.

"Then one day I heard this horse whinnying, back in the woods behind the power house. I went to investigate. Your aunt had this mare tied to a tree, the same mare that threw her later on. The horse must have tried to throw her that day, or maybe scrape her off on a tree trunk. Anyway, your aunt had unearthed a long bull whip from someplace, and she was beating the mare."

I pictured Aunt Evelyn, tall and strong in jodhpurs and shirt, face pale with fury as she lashed the plunging, screaming animal.

"I saw red. I took the whip away from her and broke its handle over my knee." He stopped for a moment, and then went on, "I've never seen such rage in a human face as I saw in hers. She started screaming at me. Then I realized we weren't alone. I looked around and saw Mrs. Escobar and Lorena standing there, and Kevin.

"She stopped screaming. She told the others to go away. Then she smiled. You know that smile of hers?"

"I know it."

"She smiled and said, 'You can go, too, Harley.'

120

"A week passed. She didn't fire me, and that worried me, because I couldn't figure out why. Now I know. She didn't want to let me off that easy. She wanted to make me really pay for humiliating her in front of her servants, and she couldn't think of just how to do it. Then Lisa handed her the chance on a silver platter."

I said, after a moment, "That bracelet?"

"Yes. Lisa stole it, all right. I'm not sure how Amy Warren found out, but probably she came slipping along that second-floor balcony the next night, while my fool of a sister was trying on the bracelet in front of the mirror. Anyway, your aunt got the bracelet back. Then she called me in and told me she was going to have Lisa arrested for grand theft."

"Could she do that? After all, she'd recovered the bracelet."

"That makes no difference. The bracelet had been stolen, and there was a witness to testify that she'd seen it in Lisa's possession."

I waited, with a cringing sense that I already knew what had happened next.

"Then she said, 'Of course, if I were married to you, maybe I wouldn't prosecute, not unless Lisa steals something else.' I asked her why in hell she'd want to marry me, and she said, 'Oh, don't worry, Joseph. You'll still be just the caretaker. But when you and I stand before the justice of the peace over in Galton Beach, you'll know what it is to be humiliated. You'll know it in spades. And for as many months as I choose to stay married to you, you'll go on knowing it. Every time you drive across the causeway for supplies, you'll know that the shopkeepers and those bums lounging on the hotel steps are snickering about the kept man, the big brave bomber pilot who married a woman old enough to be his mother. And don't think you can take your thieving sister and slip away from here. The minute you do, I'll issue a warrant for her arrest.' "

I said slowly, "I don't understand her. I should think she'd realize that they'd be snickering at her, too."

"I pointed that out to her. She said, 'I don't give a damn what that Galton Beach scum thinks of me, or what anybody thinks. All I care about is what happens on this island. Nobody whose salary I pay is going to bully me, right here on my own property, and not pay for it. And you will pay for it, plenty, because you *do* care what other people think.' "

I said in a flat voice, "So you went through with it." I tried, and failed, to banish a mental picture of Harley, standing white-faced beside my smiling aunt in some dingy office in this dingy town, while a justice of the peace droned on about the powers vested in him by the state of Florida.

Harley said, "What else could I do? Because of her juvenile record, Lisa wouldn't have gotten off, even if I'd had the money to pay for a high-powered lawyer, which I didn't. She'd have gone to prison. Or probably, because of that psychiatric report on her the last time she was arrested, she'd have gone to a state hospital. And she'd have hated that even more than prison."

We sat in silence for perhaps a minute. I became aware that the bartender was down at the far end of the room saying something to the middle-aged couple. I saw them swivel on the tall stools to look, smiling, at the back of Harley's head, and at me, sitting with fingers gripped tight around the mug handle. My aunt had been so right. Not only shopkeepers and hotel-step loungers snickered, but also bartenders and their sleazy customers.

Harley said, turning his beer mug in wet circles over the scarred table top, "It's no fun to be the victim of a bad joke. But ever since last March I've been reminding myself that that was all it was, a vindicitve joke that she'd tire of soon. Then she'd file for divorce and tell Lisa and me to get the hell off her island. So I managed to get by—until you showed up."

We looked at each other. And despite the bleakness of his face, my throat tightened with happiness, and I felt the pressure of tears behind my eyes. Here in this dismal little bar, with a nasal-voiced tenor wailing about his bad luck in Dee-troit City, Harley had just told me he loved me.

I said, "What are you going to do?"

"I don't know. I imagine she feels less inclined than ever to end her little farce right away."

"Why?"

"Because she knows that you and I spent four days cataloguing one shell cabinet. She must find the implications of that very amusing."

"She hasn't said anything to me about it."

"Don't worry, she knows. Amy Warren must have told her." He paused, and then said, "Of course, I could go into your aunt's room some night and kill her."

"Don't! Don't say things like that, even as a joke."

He gave me a faint, grim smile. "Who said it was a joke?" Then he glanced at his watch. "Almost dinnertime. We'd better go."

We went back across the causeway through fading sunset light. When we had driven through the gate, I said, "I'll walk from here." I didn't like the thought of curious eyes watching us from a window.

"All right."

He got out and went around to my side of the pickup. I slid down into his arms and stayed there. Our kiss was prolonged, hungry, and more than a little desperate. When we finally moved apart and looked at each other through the dimming light, I could tell that he, too, felt that our first kiss should be our last one, at least until Eveleyn Dunway Clayton decided that she had evened the score.

"Good night, Jennifer."

"Good night." Turning away, I walked up the tree-lined road to the house.

Fourteen

I was waiting the next night when my mother emerged from the ramp into the airport waiting room. She had the look of a small girl on her way to a party to which she had never expected to be invited. I kissed her and then asked, "Had your dinner?"

"Yes, on the plane. How about you?"

"I had something in the coffee shop." I looked at the small green-and-black plaid suitcase she carried. "Any more luggage?"

"No, just this."

We went out to the Volkswagen in the parking lot. Mother remained silent while I maneuvered through the heavy airport traffic, but once we were out on the highway, driving north beneath a sullen gray sky, she began to ask questions.

"How is Evelyn?"

"She gets about her room on crutches now."

"That's good. But how is she otherwise?"

"I think you'll find her the same as always."

"No, I suppose people don't change much." She paused. "What's her husband like?"

"His name is Harley. His sister is on the island, too."

"But what's he like?"

"You'll see before long."

From the corner of my eye I saw her open her mouth to speak, then close it. Gratefully I thought of how my mother had never pried, not into my letters while I was growing up, nor into the diary I once kept.

"Who else is staying on the island?"

I told her of Kevin, whom she remembered as a boy from that summer when I had stayed with my aunt. "There's a Cuban housekeeper, Mrs. Escobar, and her niece. And there's Amy Warren, who's a friend of Aunt Evelyn's. Amy's into the occult—witchcraft, Tarot cards, the whole bit."

"Oh, lovely! I've always wanted to have my fortune told with Tarot cards."

So, I reflected, the Dunway sisters had something in common, after all.

Until we reached Galton Beach, we talked about the manuscripts she had sent out, and about the remaining Dunway possessions I was to catalogue. But when we started across the causeway, she fell silent, looking at the island ahead, its treetops stained with sullen sunset light, and now and then drawing a deep breath. I felt she was enjoying the remembered smell of salt water, and the tang of Dolor Island pines, and the indefinable smell of rich soil and subtropical undergrowth.

The gate stood open, as I had known it would. Earlier that evening, when Harley had opened it to let me through, I had said, "I'm going to the airport to meet my mother." He had looked at me for a long moment, his eyes holding the odd mixture of emotion that I knew must be in my own—longing, bafflement, and underneath it all a defiant happiness. He said, "I'll leave the gate open."

I was grateful for his understanding. I would not have wanted to explain to my mother who he was, and why her sister's husband was acting as gatekeeper. Soon I would have to explain it all to her, unless Aunt Evelyn saved me the task, but I didn't want to right now. Let her enjoy, as much as she could, the first hours after her return to her birthplace.

We drove up the curving road between the pines and stopped at the foot of the house steps, just behind a dark red sedan. I noticed that its left rear tire was flat. I said, turning off the ignition, "That's Dr. Satherly's car."

"Evelyn's doctor? Do you think there's something wrong with her beside her leg?"

"I doubt it," I said dryly. "She was fine this afternoon."

As we climbed the steps, I said, "I asked Mrs. Escobar to put you in the room next to mine at the front of the house."

"That's fine, dear." She added, "I used to have a room at the back, next to Evelyn's."

I didn't tell her that Amy Warren occupied that room now. We crossed the lower hall and climbed the stairs, with Mother trailing behind me to exclaim over a remembered grandfather's clock and a stair carpet unfamiliar to her. In her room I put her suitcase on the bed. "I'll help you get settled."

"There's not much to unpack." She was looking around her at heavy Victorian mahogany and a faded but still attractive Axminster rug. "Funny, I don't ever remember being in this room." Then: "Did Evelyn say she would see me tonight?"

"Yes. Oh, before I forget. You were right about her will, Mother. You're her heir, and after you, me."

"I knew it. I knew Evelyn wouldn't leave her property away from her own flesh and blood."

"Suppose you freshen up while I unpack. I'll go with you to her room, and then leave you two alone."

About ten minutes later we moved along the broad, silent hall. As we neared Aunt Evelyn's door, it opened and Dr. Satherly came out, black bag in hand. I made the introduction and then said, "How is Aunt Evelyn?"

"She's fine. She's been practicing with her crutches."

"That's good. Dr. Satherly, I'm afraid your left rear tire is flat."

His customary look of irritation deepened. "I know. I must have picked up a nail on the causeway. Fortunately I have a spare with me. I can change it in the garage. Nice to have met you, Mrs. Langley," he said, and moved toward the stairs.

I knocked on the door. Aunt Evelyn called, "Come in."

My mother took a few steps past me into the room and then halted. After a moment my aunt said, "Well, Madge, sixteen years. You haven't changed much."

"Nor have you. You look beautiful."

My mother had sounded nervous and overeager and oddly young, as if the sight of the woman across the room had swept her back to some insecure time before she had acquired a husband, and brief fame, and a daughter. As the two women looked at each other, I had a sense of the room filling with memories and emotions from a time before I was on this earth. I said, stepping back into the hall, "Well, I'll leave you two now."

In my room I tried to settle down to mending the loose hem of a skirt, but I felt restless, uneasy. Crossing to the dresser, I switched on my transistor radio, and then returned to the chair and my mending. A local newscaster finished talking about a fire in St. Petersburg, and then said, "And now for the weather. Hurricane Ethrelda, now almost stationary south of Haiti, poses no immediate threat to Cuba or the Florida coast. But an area of low barometric pressure extends on all sides of the huge storm, bringing clouds and high humidity to northern Florida. A hurricane watch is in effect as far north as central Georgia. Locally we can expect more of the same tomorrow, cloudy skies and temperature in the high eighties. And now back to your favorite disk jockey, Country Bob."

Low barometer, I thought. That might account for my sense of ill ease. I got up to tune the radio lower, and then went on sewing.

Perhaps ten minutes passed. And then, through the twanging guitars of the Bluegrass Four, I heard the muffled sound of high, angry voices. As I laid my sewing aside, I realized I had been expecting something like this. I moved out into the hall thinking, "I should never have suggested that she come down here."

I had almost reached Aunt Evelyn's door when the one next to it opened and Amy Warren, an excited little smile on her lips, slipped out into the hall. At sight of me the smile died, and her face assumed a suitably distressed expression. She said in a low voice, "This is awful! We must do something."

I could hear my mother's voice distinctly now. "That's not true, Evelyn! And it's a filthy, filthy thing to say!"

I grasped Amy's elbow. Surprised, she allowed me to lead her several steps toward the stairwell before she halted and pulled back. I said, "It's none of our business."

She looked back over her shoulder. No doubt she regretted the impulse which had led her to step into the hall rather than onto the balcony. "Leave them alone," I said through the sound of my aunt's raised voice. "Let's go down to the library. There's something in William James I want to ask you about."

"But I really think someone should—"

"No, Aunt Evelyn would be furious with you if you interfered, or if she even knew we'd listened."

I could tell that thought had not struck her. "All right," she said reluctantly.

As we descended the stairs, I could still hear quarreling voices. I could hear them faintly even in the library, where I took William James down from a shelf and engaged Amy in an unwilling discussion of James's comments upon St. Theresa of Avila. Could Kevin and Lisa hear? Undoubtedly, if they were not out someplace.

And then I heard the muffled slam of a door and the sound of feet running along the upper hall toward the eastern end of the house. I closed the book. "Excuse me," I said. Not waiting to see if she followed, I moved swiftly through the dining room and out into the hall. I heard the sound of a car moving around the corner of the house. Dr. Satherly's, I thought. And then I saw that Mrs. Escobar stood at the foot of the stairs, looking up indecisively toward the now silent second floor.

She said, "I was wondering if I should—"

"No, it's all right."

I climbed upward. Just as I rounded the curve in the stairs, I saw the door opposite the landing close. Yes, Lisa was home.

The door of my mother's room stood open. Furious tears streaming down her face, she was folding a yellow cotton dress into her suitcase. I closed the door behind me. "Mother, please!"

Stooping, she picked up a pair of fluffy blue mules from the rug. "I will not sleep under this roof."

"Mother, what happened?"

She put the slippers in the suitcase lid pocket and then said, with an attempt at dignity, "There are some things a woman can't discuss with her own child. I know I'm old-fashioned, but that's the way I feel about it."

"All right. But you can't leave tonight. Probably there are no planes this late. And the hotel in Galton Beach looks pretty awful. Of course, I could drive you to St. Augustine."

She said in a subdued voice, "No, now that I think of it, I wouldn't want you driving back alone this time of night."

"Then wait until morning. You won't have to see her again. You won't even have to stay for breakfast. We'll have it on the way to the airport." I would sign over Aunt Evelyn's check to her, and make her take it.

"All right," she said. "There's a plane at eight-thirty in the morning." She didn't suggest that I fly north with her, and I was glad. What with the money she had spent on her disastrous trip down here, we were both

131

going to need those salary checks from Aunt Evelyn.

She took the slippers from the suitcase and then stood there with them in her hand. "Things started off all right. She had me open the safe and read her will, and we talked about that for a while. But then she started in about your father, and soon I was screaming at her." She paused and then said in a flat voice, "I should never have come here."

"It was my fault."

"No, Jenny. For years I've been wanting to come home."

I kissed her cheek. "I'll set my alarm for six-thirty. Try to get some sleep."

I left her and moved toward my own room. I had already opened my door when Kevin's door opened. He said, limping toward me, "Quite a sisterly reunion, eh? It sounded like nitro and glycerine coming together."

"Kevin, it's not funny."

"No, I suppose not. Anything I can do?"

I shook my head. "Good night," I said, and closed the door.

For a long time I lay awake, listening to the tick of my traveling clock and the subdued hum of the air conditioner. Despite the room's coolness, I seemed to feel the full weight of the humid night pressing down on me, and this silent, darkened house and all its other occupants. My furious, tearful mother. My aunt, perhaps not furious at all by now, and surely not tearful. I had a vision of her sitting up in bed, classic nostrils dilating, not just with exhaled cigarette smoke, but with the satisfaction of old scores paid off. I thought of Amy, wakeful with frustrated curiosity, and of Kevin, who seemed to regard everything, including tonight's emotional storm, as material for humor, and of self-centered Lisa, who probably by now had fallen into the sound sleep of the tough-minded and healthy-bodied.

And then I thought of Harley. Somehow I was sure that he, too, lay awake, down there in the cottage beside the gate, and that he was thinking of me and of Evelyn Dunway Clayton's bad joke, the legal bond which had not only humiliated him for the past four months, but which kept us at least temporarily apart.

I don't know how much sleep I got. But when the alarm brought me back to consciousness and gray morning light, I knew it had not been enough.

I had finished dressing and was hanging up my robe and nightgown, when someone knocked.

Mrs. Escobar stood out in the hall, her pale face struggling for calm. "Something has happened, Miss Langley. You'd better come with me."

Fifteen

Automatically obedient, I stepped out into the hall. "What is it?"

"It's Mrs. Clayton."

My aunt had appeared in excellent health when I had accompanied my mother to her room only hours before. And so it must have been something in Mrs. Escobar's face that made me say, in a flat voice, "She's dead."

Mrs. Escobar nodded. "Someone . . ." She broke off. "You'd better see."

With a strange, high-pitched ringing in my ears, I followed her along the hall, past my mother's closed door, and Kevin's, and Lisa's, and Amy Warren's. Mrs. Escobar grasped the knob of my aunt's door and then turned to look at me. Through my shock and dread, I felt a stir of admiration for the Cuban woman's self-control.

"She looked quite—terrible, and so I pulled the sheet up."

She opened the door, and I stepped past her into the room. The draperies had been pulled back at the long windows opening onto the balcony, and the shorter ones in the room's western wall. Gray morning light showed me a breakfast tray, laden with a silver coffee pot and rack of toast and a covered dish, which had been placed on a small folding table perhaps five feet from the sheet-covered figure on the bed.

Mrs. Escobar had followed me into the room "The draperies were drawn when I brought her breakfast. I put the tray down and opened the draperies. It wasn't until then that I saw what had happened." She paused and then added, "I don't know what the police will say about my pulling up that sheet. It seemed—indecent not to."

The police. Somehow those words made this quiet room and the sheeted figure on the bed seem unreal to me, like something out of a dream that had not yet taken a nightmare turn, but would.

I said, "Are you sure she's—"

"I'm sure. Her head is battered in. Whoever did it must have used that brass candlestick at the other side of the bed. I didn't touch it."

On legs that felt made of wood, I walked around to the other side of the bed. A bare right arm, fist clinched, dangled from beneath the sheet toward the Aubusson carpet. On the carpet lay the candlestick, the tall brass one which had stood on the highboy, its base now covered with dried red stains.

And then, with a sickening leap of the pulse in the hollow of my throat, I saw something else—the raveled edge of a scrap of cloth clutched the dead fist—light blue cloth with a narrow white stripe.

Among the clothing I had taken from my mother's suitcase the night before and hung in the closet, there had been a light blue cotton robe with a white stripe.

Almost certainly Mrs. Escobar, in the first shock of her discovery, had not noticed that bit of cloth. How could I get it away before she did see it?

Aware of my thudding heartbeats, I turned around, my body still screening the candlestick and that clenched fist from the housekeeper's view. "Mrs. Escobar, do you know Dr. Satherly's number?"

"Yes."

"Will you ask him to come here?" Ask him to notify the police, too."

As she started toward the bedside phone, I said quickly, "It's better not to touch anything in here. And I don't think you should use the phone in the upstairs hall, do you? As long as the others aren't awake, there'll be less confusion."

From the odd look she gave me, I knew she found my reason a weak one. But all she said was, "I'll use the downstairs phone."

I forced myself to wait until a second or two after I could no longer hear her quiet footsteps. Surely she was halfway down the stairs by now—unless I had aroused her suspicion, unless she was coming back along the hall, very softly. . . .

Aware of sweat rolling down my sides, I waited perhaps another thirty seconds. Then I dropped to my knees. Reaching across that bloodied candlestick, I made myself touch those clenched fingers. They were cold and quite stiff. Fighting down nausea, I pried them open. I thrust the scrap of cloth in my skirt pocket and started to stand up. Then I dropped back to my knees.

Fingerprints. There might be fingerprints on the candlestick's shaft. Get them off. I looked at the sheet. No, no. I might leave a smear of not quite dried blood. Better use a washcloth, a wet one.

Rising, I moved quickly and quietly into the bathroom. Above all, I must not wake Amy Warren. I twisted the hot water faucet in the basin ever so slightly. From the towel rack I took a fluffy white washcloth and held it under water that trickled out with agonizing slowness.

Footsteps in the hall. I shut off the water, dropped the washcloth onto the rack, and hurried into the bedroom. When Mrs. Escobar appeared in the doorway, a big key ring holding at least a dozen keys in her hand, I was standing well away from the bathroom door.

"Dr. Satherly said he'd phone the police and then drive over here. He also said we'd better lock this room until the police come." I searched my mind for some reasonable-sounding objection, and found none. But better say something. She was looking at me oddly again, and I had an absurd but terrifying sense that if her gaze dropped to my pocket, she would see right through it to that scrap of cloth. I said, "I suppose he's right."

She crossed the room and locked the long windows which led out onto the balcony. Then we moved out into the hall. She closed the door on the room's silent occupant. Sharply but helplessly aware of that candlestick lying there, I watched her turn the key in the lock. There were no fingerprints on that candlestick, I told myself. Or if there were, they were not my mother's. Despite her outraged fury, she would not have slipped out of her room sometime during the night, and entered the room of her sleeping sister, and picked up that candlestick. It was unthinkable that she would do that. And yet, that scrap of cloth in my pocket . . .

As we approached the head of the stairs, I said, "I'll wake my mother now."

"All right. There will be breakfast in the dining room soon. I took the tray up to your aunt's room first. Last night she told me she wanted an early breakfast."

As she started down the stairs, I turned my head to look after her. Despite my own anxiety, I wondered fleetingly what she felt behind that calm exterior. Shock? Horror? Or a grim satisfaction in the death of that woman who had so arbitrarily decided the fate of a retarded servant girl's child?

I moved to my mother's door and stood motionless for a moment. Then I drew a deep breath and knocked.

Quick footsteps inside. The door opened. My mother stood there, clothed in the beige linen dress and coat in which she had alighted from the plane the night before. Looking past her shoulder, I saw the plaid suitcase standing on the floor at the foot of the bed.

She said, "I was just coming to wake you. I thought I'd let you sleep as late as possible." As I stepped past her into the room, she went on, "So I got dressed and packed."

"Mother, we can't leave this morning."

"Can't leave! Jenny, I told you. I won't stay another night in that woman's—"

"Something's happened." I put my arm around her waist and drew her, resisting slightly, across the room. "You'd better sit down."

She sank onto the edge of the bed and looked up at

me, her face apprehensive now. "Mother, Aunt Evelyn is dead."

She said incredulously, "Dead! She can't be. Except for her leg, she was fine last night. Evelyn has always been as healthy as—"

"Mother, she's dead. Someone came into her room last night and used a candlestick to—to—"

"Oh, my God!" She buried her face in her hands.

I looked down at the honey-blond hair, the small shoulders that had begun to tremble. Then my gaze went to the suitcase at the foot of the bed. I had to get into that suitcase.

And if inside it I found a blue-and-white striped cotton robe with a small piece torn out of it? Then I would get rid of it, I thought grimly. Bury it somewhere in the woods, or walk out onto the dock at the northern end of the island tonight and drop it, well weighted with rocks, into several feet of water. Whether I was right or wrong, the one thing I would not do was to turn evidence against my own mother over to the police.

I put my hand on her shoulder. "Mother, come downstairs. There's breakfast in the dining room."

She took her hands down from her face. It was wet, and her eye make-up had run. She looked at least ten years older than the smiling, eager woman who had stepped off the plane the night before. "Oh, Jenny. I couldn't."

"You should. At the very least, you should have coffee." I had to get her downstairs so that I could slip back up here and open that suitcase before the police came. Probably they would not look through the bedrooms, at least not right away. But they might. And if they found a torn robe or—a terrible thought which had not occurred to me until then—one stained with Evelyn Clayton's blood . . .

"All right. I'll have to wash my face first." She wiped the back of her hand across one cheek. There was something so touchingly childlike in the gesture that I hated myself for thinking she could possibly have wielded that candlestick. Nevertheless, all my anxiety surged back as I waited impatiently, seated on the bed, and watched her go into the bathroom, wash and dry her face, pick up a mascara stick, put it down again, and then come back into the bedroom.

I got to my feet. "Well, let's go down." Then quickly, as she reached for her satchel handbag of beige leather on the dressing table: "You won't need that."

Her suitcase key was probably in her handbag.

Obediently, she set the bag down. We left the room.

Sixteen

Down in the dining room I found that I, too, had no appetite for the buffet's offering of eggs, sausages, and toast. After I had poured two cups of coffee, my mother and I sat with our chairs close together at the long table. She seemed too dazed to ask questions, and I was thankful for that.

I was about to make an excuse—the need for a handkerchief—to slip upstairs, when I heard the sound I had dreaded—the doorbell's chime. Through the archway I caught a glimpse of Mrs. Escobar hurrying to answer. I heard her voice, and those of at least two men, and then the approach of several footsteps.

Three men in khaki trousers and shirts halted politely in the archway. One of them said, " 'Morning, ladies. I'm Sheriff Bixby, from over in Galton Beach." He was about fifty, a lean man with graying red hair. With his Florida drawl and prominent Adam's apple, he might have seemed a stereotype of the small-town sheriff, except for the gray eyes set under jutting brow ridges. They held such alert intelligence that my nerves stretched even tighter.

"I'm Jennifer Langley, Mrs. Clayton's niece. And this is my mother, Mrs. Langley."

He looked at her. "Mrs. Clayton's sister?"

She swallowed before she spoke. "Yes."

"My sympathy to both you ladies."

I nodded an acknowledgment.

"I've asked the lady who let us in to get the rest of the people in the house together. Is there someplace quiet where we can have a little talk after a while?"

"The library's through there."

He crossed to the library doorway, looked in, and then said, turning around, "That'll do fine. You ladies can wait in there after you've finished your breakfast. No, no rush. I'll leave Deputy Saunders here"—he nodded toward a fat, blond man of about thirty—"to keep you company."

Translation: to keep an eye on you.

"Well, George, let's go upstairs." He nodded to Mother and me, and then, with his other deputy, a bald, husky-looking man of early middle age, turned toward the stairs.

I said to the fat man, "Will you have some coffee?"

"Thanks, miss. Coffee would go good about now." He poured himself a cup, sat down at the table, and then seemed to go off into a reverie, light blue gaze fixed on the windows, right hand raising the cup at intervals to take an audible sip. I looked at my mother, and she nodded, white-faced. We got up and went into the library.

At this early hour of an overcast morning, only a little light penetrated the shrubbery crowding against the

142

windows. I turned on the chandelier, and then sat down near the étagère of seashells. Fleetingly I thought of Harley. Had anyone told him yet? Then again I was conscious of nothing but my mother's huddled presence, and that scrap of cloth in my pocket, and the muffled tramp of feet in that corner bedroom directly overhead.

Twice again the doorbell sounded, each time followed by the distant sound of masculine feet on the stairs. The state police? Men from the coroner's office?

The doorbell rang again. I heard someone go up the stairs and then, after an interval, come down them at a rapid pace. The deputy's chair scraped over the floor in the dining room. I heard voices, first out in the hall, then in the next room. "Sorry, Doc. Sheriff's orders. Nobody who shows up can leave until he has a chance to talk to them. You'll have to wait with the ladies in there."

Dr. Satherly came into the room, black bag in hand, face mottled with angry red. He said loudly, standing a few feet inside the doorway, "This is an outrage. That fool of a sheriff won't even let me in upstairs. And now I can't leave. And I've got calls to—"

He broke off as Kevin and Lisa came into the room. Kevin said, looking around him, "Now isn't this one hell of a note?" He was pale under his tan, and his voice held none of its usual lazy amusement.

Lisa said, "Aren't you going to have breakfast, Kevin?" She looked as cool and indifferent as ever, but I detected a note of strain in her voice.

Kevin said, "God, no."

"Well, I am." She turned and went into the dining room, almost colliding with Amy Warren.

Amy said, gray eyes behind the butterfly glasses moving from one face to another, "Isn't it dreadful? A terrible, terrible shock." I saw that however shocked she had been, she had taken time to arrange her graying brown hair carefully, and apply lipstick. "And to think I went on sleeping, right in the next room, while poor Evelyn— You're Evelyn's sister, aren't you?"

My mother said, with obvious effort, "Yes. And you must be Mrs. Warren."

"That's right. Evelyn was my dearest friend. Who could have done this awful thing?"

Kevin, lounging in the doorway, evidently was feeling more like himself again, because he said, "That should be no problem for you. Just go into a trance and ask one of your spooks."

She threw him a furious look. Then she sat down with a dignified air and folded her hands in her lap. No one spoke until Harley appeared in the doorway. He paused there for a moment, gaze locked with mine. Suddenly I recalled how he had said, in that Galton Beach bar, "Of course, I could slip into her room some night and kill her." It had been nothing but a bitter joke, of course. But was he also remembering those words now?

I said, "Mother, this is Harley Clayton." He came across the room to take the hand she offered. From her face, which did not change its dazed expression, I could not be sure that his name had even registered.

"Sorry to keep you waiting, folks." I looked at the doorway and saw Sheriff Bixby standing there. Mrs. Escobar and Lorena stood a half pace behind him. "Please sit down, everybody." He turned his head to look at the housekeeper and her niece. "You too, ladies."

He walked to the head of the long library table,

waited until everyone was seated, and then said quickly, as if wanting to get that part of it over with, "Mrs. Clayton's body has been removed."

Along the rear balcony, I thought, and down those side stairs. By now an ambulance might be speeding across the causeway, carrying the body of the woman who for a quarter of a century had ruled over this little island and the destinies of everyone on it.

The sheriff's gaze was going around the room. "Now I think I know who all of you are, from what Mrs. Escobar has told me. You've all been staying on the island except Dr. Satherly here."

"Exactly!" Dr. Satherly said. "And so I see no reason why I should be detained here now."

"You were here last night, weren't you?"

"Yes, calling on my patient! I had to change a flat tire afterwards, but I left the island around eleven-thirty."

The sheriff's gaze went to Harley. "You occupy the gatehouse, don't you?"

So Mrs. Escobar had told him of the strange living arrangements of my aunt and the man who was legally her husband. Harley nodded, his face stony.

"Can you confirm what Dr. Satherly says?"

"No. I didn't open the gate for him."

"I have my own key to the gate!" Dr. Satherly's voice had turned a little shrill. "Evelyn—Mrs. Clayton—gave it to me years ago, so that in an emergency I could get to her without any delay."

"Well, all right. Now we've got to try to find out who was the last person to see Mrs. Clayton alive."

"I suppose I was," Mrs. Escobar said. "I waited up, as usual. She rang for me about one o'clock, and I helped her undress."

One o'clock! And she'd had to be up before six. Again I wondered what she was feeling behind that calm, plump face.

Kevin said, "Look, sheriff, before you keep us all cooped up here, don't you think you ought to tell us whether or not you have any idea who did this?"

Sheriff Bixby frowned, and then said mildly, "If I did, I'd have made an arrest on suspicion."

Kevin grinned. "Score one for you. But can you tell us whether you've found any fingerprints? Mrs. Escobar said that whoever killed Mrs. Clayton had used a candlestick."

My stomach knotted a little more tightly. Sheriff Bixby shot the housekeeper a slightly annoyed look. Had he told her not to mention the candlestick? Or had he forgotten to tell her? "There's a man upstairs testing for fingerprints right now. All right, let's get on with it. Did anything unusual happen here last night? Earlier, I mean."

There was a brief silence. Then Amy Warren said, "I'm sorry, Mrs. Langley. I'm sorry, Jennifer, but I'll have to speak out. Evelyn's sister, Mrs. Langley, arrived here last night, and she and Evelyn had a terrible quarrel in Evelyn's room. Her daughter heard it, and so did Mrs. Escobar. I saw her at the foot of the stairs listening."

The sheriff turned to my mother. "Well, Mrs. Langley?"

She looked so small sitting there, so helpless. I wanted to put my hand over the ones she held clenched in her lap, but I knew it would be best not to appear too concerned, and so I sat still.

"Yes, my sister and I did have a—a terrible fight."

"What about?"

"My—my husband."

"Your husband? Where is he?"

"He's dead! He was killed in a hit-and-run accident almost sixteen years ago. But Evelyn said that the only way I could have gotten him away from her was to—was to—"

"Yes, Mrs. Langley?"

"She said he must have felt he had to marry me! And that's not true!" She turned to me. "You know it's not, Jenny. You remember that you weren't born until four years after your father and I were married."

The strain must have addled my mind, because I said, "No, I don't exactly remember it, but—"

Kevin let out a guffaw, and even Dr. Satherly smiled. The sheriff said, "We know what you meant, Mrs. Langley. Now how was your sister when you left her? All right?"

My mother looked at him, lips slightly parted. "Of course she was all right. She wasn't even angry by then. I was the one who was still furious. But surely you don't think that I—"

"I'm not thinking anything just yet, Mrs. Langley. I'm just trying to gather a little background. Now let's get to Mrs. Clayton's will. Does anyone know anything about that?"

There was no help for it. He would find out sooner or later. I said, "She showed me her will. It's in the safe, behind a still-life painting near the bedroom door. The combination is pasted to the underside of the drawer in a small table near the bed."

"Do you know if there's anything else in the safe?"

"A case. A jewelry case, I suppose."

"And what does her will say?"

"She left five thousand to her husband." I didn't look at Harley. "Everything else goes to my mother. I was named as the beneficiary in the event my mother died before she did."

"I suppose there's a copy of the will with her lawyer."

"I don't think so. It's a holograph will. She said it was the best kind, because it needed no witnesses and no lawyer."

"Lots of people have that idea, and it's true in some states. But holograph wills aren't recognized in Florida. Still, probate courts take such wills into consideration when they make their decision." He looked at my mother. "Did you know about her will?"

My mother's face held something besides shocked distress now. I recognized it as growing apprehension. "Yes. Before we—before the quarrel started, she had me open the safe and read the will."

"Excuse me, folks." He raised his voice. "Johnny!"

The fat blond deputy came into the room. "You take over here for a couple of minutes. I'm going upstairs."

When the sheriff had gone, his deputy sat down at one end of the long table and stared over our heads. After glancing at him, I fixed my gaze on the floor, too wretchedly aware of the candlestick upstairs and of that torn scrap in my pocket to look at anyone. In the silence I heard the distant roar of a jet, and wondered if it was the north-bound plane my mother had intended to take.

Sheriff Bixby came back into the room. Without being told, his deputy got up and walked out. Standing at the head of the table, the sheriff sent a sweeping look around the room and then said, "The will's not there. Neither is the jewel case."

I felt surprise, and then overwhelming relief. I said, "Then there's no need to ask my mother any more questions, sheriff. As the beneficiary of that will, she would never have taken it from the safe, would she?"

"Well, miss, that's one way of looking at it."

"What other way is there?"

"Well, there was this case in St. Augustine a few years back. Two business partners, one an old bachelor, the other a widower with no children. They made wills in each other's favor. Then the bachelor, in a fit of rage, killed the other fellow. Guess he wasn't thinking clear afterwards, because he opened their office safe and destroyed both wills, to try to make the police think he had no motive. It was sort of stupid, because their lawyer had a copy of both wills. But here we've got a hand-written will, with no copies. So suppose this little lady got so steamed up last night that she went back to her sister's room about two o'clock. That's when the doc from the coroner's office said it happened. Suppose she picked up that candlestick and—"

"I didn't!" My mother's voice was a wail. "How can you—"

"We're just supposing, ma'am. Now bear with me a minute. Suppose when you realized what you'd done, you remembered that will—"

"I don't care much for your way of supposing, sheriff." Harley's voice was cold. "Don't you realize it must have been someone who didn't belong on this island? Someone who killed her for the jewelry in her safe?"

"Oh, we thought of that, Mr. Clayton. With that bal-

149

cony running along the rear of the house, almost anybody could have gotten into that room from the outside. Trouble is, why would a burglar steal an envelope
with a will in it?"

"Why not?" Harley said. "He might have thought
there were stock certificates in it."

I looked at his taut face. Was he trying to help my
mother? Or was it his sister he was trying to protect?
Lisa, who sat over there with her long bare legs crossed
and her arms folded across her striped jersey, listening
to the conversation with an air of slightly contemptuous calm. Lisa, who in the past had shown herself to
be quite capable of appropriating other people's property.

Or could it be—the thought was as inevitable as it
was unwelcome—that Harley needed to protect
himself? With all the justification in the world, he had
hated my aunt. And then, feeling sick, I realized that
the police might think he had another reason. That
will. Now that it was gone, now that there was only
mine and my mother's statement to indicate it had ever
existed, the dead woman's husband stood an excellent
chance of inheriting her estate.

Surely that thought had occurred to Sheriff Bixby. I
waited for him to put it into words. But all he said was,
"Yes, we figured that a burglar might think he was getting securities."

"Of course he might have," Harley said. "And there
have been strangers on this island. Miss Langley saw
one just the other night."

"That right, miss?" I nodded. "Get a good look at
him, enough so you could recognize him or a picture of
him?"

"I'm sure I could."

"All right. I'll ask you for a description later on. Any of the rest of you see this fellow?"

"I think I heard him," Kevin said. "At least I heard a power boat pulling away from the dock. The next day Harley strung barbed wire around the dock, but still someone with wire cutters . . ."

The sheriff nodded. "We'll take a good look around the island. Haven't had time yet. Well, I guess that's—" He broke off, looking at a man who had appeared in the doorway—a thin little man of about fifty-five in a rumpled dark suit. "Yes, Charlie?"

The man shook his head. "All right, Charlie. I'll see you outside."

The man turned away. Kevin said into the brief silence, "So. No fingerprints on the candlestick."

The sheriff looked annoyed. Then he said, "That's right. No prints on the candlestick." I don't know whether or not my profound relief showed in my face, but if so, Sheriff Bixby did not seem to notice it. He went on, "But I'm sure Charlie Walmsey got plenty of prints elsewhere in that room. Probably all of them belong to you people here in the household. But there might be an odd one, and if I get real lucky, it might match up with a police photo of that stranger Miss Langley saw. Anyway, Walmsey will be back here tomorrow or the next day to take all of your prints."

"Well," he concluded, "I guess that's all for now, except that I'll have to ask all of you to stick around pretty close for a while."

Dr. Satherly said in an outraged voice, "You mean I have to stay here? What about my practice?"

"Of course you don't have to stay. And the rest of

you may need to go over to the mainland for one reason or another, or maybe even to St. Augustine. I just meant—well, if any of you were planning a trip to Miami or New York or someplace, you'll have to postpone it. That's all for now. Sorry to have kept you so long."

He walked from the room. Under cover of the talk and movement all around us, I said in a low voice, "Mother, let's go upstairs."

We slipped out of the room. At the head of the stairs she halted and looked to her left, toward the closed door of Aunt Evelyn's room. "Come on," I said.

In her room she went over to the window and stood looking out over the front lawn. I stayed near the foot of the bed, conscious of that suitcase only inches from my leg. She said, not turning, "There used to be a big live oak right in the center of the lawn. Do you remember it?"

"Yes. It died, I guess."

"Is that funny old pavilion still in the woods?"

"Yes. Mother, why don't you go and look at it? I didn't have a shower this morning, so I'll take a quick one and then join you there."

She said in a muffled voice, "I suppose a walk would do me good."

Almost as soon as the door had closed behind her, I opened the beige handbag. Yes, there was the key in a zippered side pocket. Aware of my racing heartbeats, I hoisted the suitcase onto the bed and unlocked it.

The folded dressing gown was the third garment from the top. I held it up. With a relief that left me weak and shaking, I saw that there were no hideous red stains, and no tear. I took the scrap of cloth from my pocket. It was a lighter blue than the robe, I saw now, and its white stripe was narrower.

In Lisa's room, or Amy's, or downstairs in Mrs. Escobar's and Lorena's living quarters, was there a robe with a piece torn from it? Well, not my business to find out. I'd just turn the scrap over to the sheriff. I might find myself in trouble as a result, but surely not too much trouble. Sheriff Bixby had seemed like a nice man. Surely he would understand why I had waited until I could look into this suitcase.

Then a thought held me motionless. I had been so intent upon inspecting the robe that it had not occurred to me that the scrap could have been torn from another sort of garment. A dress. A skirt. A woman's shirt. Or a man's.

Harley.

Crossing through the bathroom, I placed the bit of cloth under the paper which lined my top bureau drawer. I went back to my mother's room, hung her clothes in the closet, and shoved the empty suitcase under the bed. Then I went down the stairs, past the dining room where Mrs. Escobar and Lorena were placing covered dishes on the buffet, and out into the muggy, overcast day.

When I turned onto the path leading to the pavilion, I saw my mother sitting on its concrete steps. She got up and moved toward me. How could I have feared for even a moment . . . "I unpacked for you," I said, and then bent and kissed her cheek soundly.

Her shaky smile widened. "What was that for?"

"Oh, because I sort of like you."

"I don't like myself," she said, and burst into tears. "She said awful things to me," she sobbed, "but I said awful things back. I wish I hadn't. My only sister! And just a few hours later—"

"Try not to think about it now." I put my arms around her shoulders. "Come on. Let's go look at the ocean."

Seventeen

All the rest of that long day—while I sat with my mother on the sand looking at the gray water, and returned with her for a belated lunch in the deserted dining room, and then went upstairs to try, unsuccessfully, to immerse myself in the Jane Austen novel—all that time, I toyed with the idea of finding some excuse not to go down to the dinner table that night. A headache would do. And with the others downstairs I might find time for a quick search of Amy's room, and Lisa's, and even Kevin's.

Finally I abandoned the idea. My reason was based partly on logic and partly on sheer cowardice. Unless he or she was in a very distraught state indeed, whoever had killed my aunt must be aware by now that he had left a torn scrap of clothing—left it in the dead woman's hand, or on the floor beside the bed. (Had she been asleep when her killer entered that room? Probably. I imagined her, just before the first blow fell, coming awake to grapple with her assailant in the dark, an assailant who tore himself from her grasp to bring that candlestick down again and again.) Probably hours before the body was discovered, that torn robe—or skirt, or shirt—had been hidden far too securely for a hasty search of mine to uncover it.

Besides, even the thought of such a search sent ripples of fear down my body. The owner of that torn garment had already committed one brutal murder, and in cold blood. I pictured myself searching through a rack of cheap, fussy dresses in Amy's closet, or an array of shorts and chinos and blue jeans in Lisa's, or a drawerful of Kevin's shirts—only to hear the door open and turn to see the room's owner and know, from the leap of fear and rage in that person's eyes, that my aunt's killer stood only a few feet from me.

No, let the sheriff handle it. Let the police try to find that torn garment and determine whether it belonged to an occupant of this house, or to Dr. Satherly, or to some unknown thief many miles away from here by now. Yes, I'd turn over that scrap of cloth to Sheriff Bixby.

But not yet. Not until I had made sure that there was no torn blue shirt with a white stripe in the care-taker's cottage. I didn't know how I would make sure, but I would.

At six o'clock I crossed the connecting bath and softly opened my mother's door. In the blue robe that had given me so much anxiety, she lay asleep atop the coverlet. Let her sleep, I thought. After what she had been through, she needed all the rest she could get.

I had returned to my room and picked up *Emma,* when someone knocked. I found Mrs. Escobar out in the hall with Sheriff Bixby beside her. He said, "Mind if I come in for a few minutes? I'd like to get that description now."

"Of course."

He nodded to Mrs. Escobar and then came into the room, closing the door behind him. While I perched on the edge of the bed, he sat down in the armchair and took a paper-covered notebook and the stub of a yellow pencil from the pocket of his khaki shirt. "By the way," he said, "it looks like maybe a trespasser was on the island last night. We found that barbed wire cut all to smithereens."

I said with vast relief, "Then it must have been some stranger—"

"Begins to look that way."

I felt an impulse to cross to the bureau, take that cloth scrap from under the drawer lining, and hand it to him. A moment later I was glad I had not, because he said casually, "Of course, anybody who lives here could just as well have cut that wire. There's a pair of wire cutters in the garage."

I said in a strained voice, "Oh, I didn't know."

"Now for your description of that man you saw."

When I had finished describing the man with the scar, Sheriff Bixby said, "You're a good observer. I wish everyone was. It'd make our job a lot easier." He paused. "How's your mother?"

"All right. She's asleep now."

"She looks like a nice little lady. Sorry if I seemed rough on her this morning. But she had had that row with Mrs. Clayton. And sometimes we find it best to bear down on somebody who's already upset. We're apt to get more information that way."

"I suppose so."

He rose. "Well, thank you, Miss Langley."

I, too, got up. "Do the others know about that cut barbed wire?"

"Yes. At least I told Mrs. Escobar, and that young fellow with the limp. What's his name, Shaughnessy? In fact, he was the one who showed me the wire cutters in the garage." He paused. "But as I told him and the housekeeper, we're still asking everybody to stick around. Well, good-by, Miss Langley."

When the gong sounded more than an hour later, my mother and I went down to the dining room. I had expected that Lisa would avoid the dinner table that night, and that Kevin and Amy Warren might, too. They did not. Perhaps each feared that by not appearing, he or she might arouse suspicion in the rest.

The funeral, Amy announced, would be held at three o'clock on Wednesday in a St. Augustine chapel. The services would be strictly private—a stipulation that must have been designed, I realized, to keep out the morbidly curious, since so few people would have any other reason to attend. "Upset as I was," Amy said, "I knew someone would have to arrange things for poor Evelyn, so I asked Sheriff Bixby's permission, and he said to go ahead." Her gaze turned to my mother. "I hope you don't mind, Mrs. Langley. I know it was your place to make the funeral arrangements, but you seemed so—so—"

"Not at all," my mother said vaguely. "I mean, it was very kind of you."

Mrs. Warren nodded graciously. "I'm sure," she said, looking around the table, "that we were all relieved to hear about the barbed wire. Now we can be almost sure it was some professional thief who did that terrible thing."

"But only almost," Kevin said. "Those wire cutters in the garage are pretty sharp. Even you could have sneaked down there last night and cut the wire."

His heart, though, did not seem to be in the familiar game of baiting Amy. Before she could frame an indignant reply, he turned to my mother. "I have three of your old records, Mrs. Langley."

My mother brightened. "You do? I wouldn't have thought someone your age—"

"Oh, there are quite a few of us Big Band buffs around. By the way, do you know where I could get an original recording of Duke Ellington's 'Three O'Clock Blues'?"

Soon my mother and Kevin were deep in a discussion of nineteen-forties greats—Count Basie, the Dorsey brothers, the Andrews sisters, and the young Frank Sinatra. I felt the tension around the table relax. Even Lisa seemed interested, and Amy asked my mother, with a blend of envy and malice, what it was like to be an ex-celebrity.

With my thoughts centered on that torn scrap of cloth, I said little. Would Harley go to the funeral? Yes, I thought so. Just as he had hated his role in the Vietnam War, but played it through, he would force himself to carry out this last bit of hypocrisy demanded by Aunt Evelyn's joke.

But I would stay home from the funeral. I would sprain an ankle, if I had to. And once everyone had gone from the island, I would search that cottage down by the gate.

159

Lorena, looking subdued and nervous, brought in the coffee tray and set it down before Amy Warren so awkwardly that little cups rattled. Amy frowned and then, with a gracious air, began to hand the cups around. As soon as the meal was over, Mother and I went upstairs. In her room she took a packet of playing cards from her suitcase, and I hoisted the suitcase onto the bed to serve as a card table. We sat on opposite sides of it while I dealt out cards for two-handed bridge.

"Jenny, if that will isn't found, what becomes of this island?"

"I don't know."

"It will go to Harley, won't it?"

"Probably. But if it does, I think he will refuse it. Then it will be yours."

"I think I'd sell it. I don't want it after what's happened here, do you?"

"No."

My mother looked at her hand, then laid it down. "You like Harley, don't you?"

"Yes."

Her expression made me think that she had guessed that I liked him very much. But all she said was, "I like him, too." She picked up her hand, laid it down again, and burst out, "Jenny, why did he marry Evelyn?"

"Not for the reason you would think." The reason everyone must think, including the gravediggers who would stand at a distance in that St. Augustine cemetery, hiding their ribald cynicism behind solemn faces until the blond man and the others turned away from the grave.

"Mother, it's not a nice story. Do you want to hear it

160

now? Whatever she was, she died less than twenty-four hours ago."

"No," she said after a moment, "I don't want to hear it. When I sit there at her funeral, I want to think of the nice things that happened between us, like the time she gave me half her allowance because I'd lost mine. When she chose to, Evelyn could be very generous, you know."

"I know."

She picked up her hand again, looked at it, rearranged her cards, and said, "Two hearts."

Sheriff Bixby and the rumpled-looking fingerprint man came back the next afternoon. In the library all of us, including Harley, stood in line at the long table and one by one pressed our fingers on an inky pad. It was an embarrassing procedure. Aware of the nervous little smile on my mother's face and my own, I looked at the others' faces—Harley's impassive one, and Lisa's, hiding whatever she felt behind her usual slightly contemptuous air. When it was his turn, Kevin reacted by snarling, Bogart-fashion, "the jail ain't built that can hold me, see?" to Mr. Walmsey, who did not seem amused. Mrs. Escobar appeared unwontedly ill at ease, and Lorena looked frightened out of what few wits she had.

As for Amy, she had the air of someone forced by her sense of civic duty to take part in a proceeding that was not only unpleasant but indecent. When she had pressed her fingers onto the pad and then wiped them with a tissue from the box beside it, she said, "I hope you'll remember to take Dr. Satherly's fingerprints, too."

Standing beside the man seated at the table, Sheriff Bixby said, "We already have, ma'am."

Perhaps two minutes later, after Mrs. Escobar and Lorena had pressed their fingertips to the pad, Sheriff Bixby said, "Just wait here. We're going into the next room to compare your prints with the ones we took from Mrs. Clayton's room. We'll only be a short time."

A short time turned out to be about ten uneasy minutes, during which all of us, even Kevin, remained silent, listening to the subdued murmur of voices in the next room. When the sheriff came back into the library, he was alone.

"Looks like all of you have been in Mrs. Clayton's room at one time or another."

"Speaking for myself," Amy said, "I had every good reason—"

"Ma'am, I'm sure you all had perfectly good reasons to be in that room."

"The important question is," Kevin said, "did you find a print that didn't belong to any of us?"

After a moment Bixby answered, "No, they all belonged either to you folks, or to Mrs. Clayton's doctor."

Amy said into the silence, "If you're trying to tell us that it had to be one of us—"

"I'm not. You see, more than the candlestick had been wiped clean. The handle to the long windows opening onto the balcony was, too, and the table with the combination pasted to the drawer, and the safe. See what a problem that makes for us? It could have been one of you folks who wiped out those fingerprints. Or it could have been a professional safecracker."

Why was he telling us this? A moment later I realized why. He said, his alert, genial gaze sweeping our faces, "Only trouble with the safecracker theory is that he wouldn't have needed the combination. It's a simple safe. Any pro could have opened it in five minutes just by listening to the tumblers drop. So how come that little table and its drawer were wiped clean?"

No one answered him. He said, turning toward the dining room, "Well, that'll be it for now, folks."

Kevin said, "You forgot to say, 'Stick around.'"

Bixby turned back. "That's right. Except for the funeral tomorrow, stick around," he said, and left the room.

We all moved across the dining room and out into the entrance hall. As my mother and I started up the stairs, Harley said, "Jennifer."

My mother smiled at me and went on up the stairs. Harley asked, "Are you all right?"

Standing on the third stair, I looked down at him. "Yes, I'm all right." Or at least I might be, after I had searched that cottage down by the gate tomorrow.

We stood motionless for several seconds, trying to convey with our eyes all that we wanted to say, and could not. Then, perhaps because Sheriff Bixby still lingered by the front door, gazing about him with an air of ingenuous admiration at the grandfather's clock and spiral stairs, Harley nodded to me and turned away. Better not give Bixby reason to think that Harley had some additional reason to welcome the death of the rich woman he had married.

I, too, turned away and went up the stairs.

Eighteen

At eleven-thirty the next morning I crossed the bath to my mother's room. She sat at the dressing table writing in a small notebook bound in black leather. The face she turned to me looked guilty.

"I'm jotting down another idea for revising one of those manuscripts. I know it seems awful, working on the day of my sister's funeral. But you understand, Jenny. It helps take my mind off what happened to Evelyn."

"The funeral's what I came to talk to you about. I'm not going."

"Jenny! You must."

"No. I didn't like Aunt Evelyn. I'm not going to sit there and pretend to believe someone's eulogy of her."

"But what will the others think?"

"When you go down to lunch, tell them I have an upset stomach. I'll skip lunch."

"I'll tell them you have a splitting headache. And you'll not skip lunch. You're thin as a rail already. I'll have Lorena bring something up to you."

Around two o'clock, half an hour after I had eaten the ham sandwich and green salad Lorena had brought me, I stood at the window watching the others prepare to drive to St. Augustine. Dr. Satherly, who had arrived an hour before and apparently had lunched downstairs, was at least temporarily at the head of the little cortege. He sat at the wheel of his sedan, with Mrs. Escobar and Lorena in the back seat. Behind them in the rakish MG, Kevin and Lisa, who wore a dark but mini-skirted dress, made a strange-looking pair of mourners indeed.

The third car was Aunt Evelyn's Lincoln. I saw Harley, in a dark suit, hand my mother and Amy Warren into the rear seat, and then go around to the door on the driver's side. For a moment before he opened it, he looked up at the window where I stood. I was sure that he could not see through the curtain, but I was also sure, from the look on his face, that he hoped I stood there. I wondered, feeling guilty warmth in my face, what he would think if he knew that in a little while I would invade his cottage.

He got into the Lincoln. The three cars moved along the curving drive and then entered the road that led away through the pines. Eight people, none of whom, except perhaps for Amy Warren, had much reason to mourn Evelyn Dunway Clayton. But which one of the eight, as he or she sat decorously in the chapel, would in memory move about a darkened room where a dreadfully silent figure lay, and wipe a candlestick's shaft free of fingerprints, and then the safe, and then that fragile French table? Now that I was sure it was not my mother, I did not care which of the others it was, as long as it was not Harley. And as soon as I had made sure that there was no torn blue-and-white striped garment in that little cottage, I would drive to Galton Beach and rid myself of that scrap of cloth.

I crossed to the bureau, took out the scrap, and put it in an envelope from a box of letter paper still in my suitcase. I slipped the envelope into a zippered compartment of my shoulder bag. Then I left my room and went quickly down the curving stairs through the silent house.

It was not until I was back in the garage, getting into the VW, that I realized with dismay that perhaps I could not get off the island that afternoon. Undoubtedly Harley had locked the gate, and if he did not keep an extra key in the cottage . . . Perhaps the cottage itself was locked, and I would have to try to get a window open. Well, I would cross those bridges when I came to them. I drove down through gray, sticky heat to the cottage and stopped beside it.

The high steel gate stood closed, its two wings held together by a formidable-looking padlock. I mounted the steps of the little house. Its doorknob turned easily under my hand.

No air conditioning here, and precious little insulation. I stepped into breathless heat and stood looking around a combination kitchen–living room that looked spartanly simple, and as well-scrubbed as a hospital operating room. A two-burner electric plate sat on a pine cabinet that probably contained utensils. A wall shelf above the sink held a few plates and cups. In the center of the room, beneath a paper-shaded droplight, stood a bare pine table with a worn leather armchair beside it. And that was all.

The bedroom had that same almost monklike plainness. A single bed with a wooden headboard and a worn out clean gray cotton spread. A battered oak wardrobe in lieu of a clothes closet, and an equally battered oak bureau. On the white cotton runner that covered its top there was a comb and a pair of wooden-backed brushes, laid out with military precision. There were also two framed photographs, one a studio portrait of a vaguely familiar-looking man and a young-ish woman, whom I took to be Harley's parents, and the other an enlarged snapshot of a tall blond youth and a girl about ten, with flaxen pigtails and a winning smile. Harley and Lisa, before he had gone off to war, and while she was still, in his phrase, "the nicest little kid in the world." Between the two photographs rested a pinkish-brown seashell. The same *conus sozoni* he had found that day we talked on the beach? It looked like it.

What would they think, that bartender in Galton Beach and that grinning middle-aged couple, if they could see how "the young guy who married that rich dame" lived?

No clothing in the upper bureau drawer. Just a leather traveling kit, probably holding a comb and brush and toothbrush container, a smaller leather box of the sort in which men keep shirt studs, and two flat cardboard boxes. Trying not to feel too ashamed of myself, I began to go through the lower drawers. Neatly folded undershorts and cotton T-shirts and pajamas. Pairs of socks, rolled into balls. Shirts, still with the laundry's paper bands around them. Three of the shirts were light blue, but none had a white stripe.

I turned to the wardrobe. Two pairs of blue jeans and two pairs of khaki pants, draped over hangers. A gray suit. A gray flannel robe. A narrow-lapeled brown checked sports jacket he must have bought before he went to Vietnam. No uniforms.

I opened the drawer at the base of the wardrobe. Two pairs of shoes, one black, one brown, and both with a high gloss. A pair of chukker boots. And a flat, glass-topped display case containing perhaps thirty seashells, each with its identifying label pasted beneath. Had he just not gotten around to adding that *conus sozoni* to the case? Perhaps. But I preferred to think it was because we had talked of that shell, the day when the line of pelicans had flown with grotesque grace across the sky, that he kept it on his bureau.

I went into the kitchen and opened the cabinet below the sink. Nothing but pots and pans, and, in the cabinet's drawer, worn silver-plated flatware. I looked around the hot, silent room and then, as an afterthought, went into the tiny, old-fashioned bathroom and picked up the splintered wicker hamper. As I up-ended it, underwear, socks of various colors, and two khaki shirts tumbled onto the cracked linoleum. No blue shirt with a white stripe.

I restored the laundry to the hamper and then stood there, feeling a vast relief. No point in dwelling on the thought that in this isolated place he could easily have burned it, or dropped it, well-weighted, off the causeway. No garment of that particular material was here, or had ever been here.

I glanced at my watch. A little after three. If I could find a gate key right away, I might be able to get over to the sheriff's office before the others returned.

No key in the pockets of the clothing that hung in the wardrobe. I opened the top bureau drawer. One of the flat boxes contained notepaper, the other old letters. The top envelope was addressed in a feminine hand—Lisa's?—to Captain Harley James Clayton, at an APO number. The small leather box held cuff links, buttons of various sizes and colors, and a Distinguished Flying Cross, awarded to Captain Harley James Clayton on May 9, 1970.

No duplicate key.

I took one last look around the little room. Someday I would tell him that I had invaded his house and searched through his possessions. Someday, but not right away. Leaving the bedroom, I moved across the kitchen through the hot silence.

Something pulled me to a halt. I heard a ripping sound.

I let out a startled cry. Then, even before I turned around, I realized what had happened. My shoulder bag had caught on that old leather chair's wooden-framed back. As I disengaged the strap, I saw that only one stitch held it to the bag. Well, no matter. I could have it mended, or even try to mend it myself. Clutching the bag, I went out onto the tiny front porch and closed the door.

How heavy the air was. Not a breath of wind stirred. Before I got into the VW, I looked at the flat gray water stretching toward the mainland, and then up at the sullen sky. Ethrelda? Perhaps. After sitting well south of Cuba for several days, churning on its center, the giant storm might have started to move.

As I drove up between rows of pines that stood absolutely motionless, I turned on the car radio. A voice said, "—as far north as Cape May. Locally, residents of low-lying areas are urged to seek higher ground. This message just in: the county chapter of the Red Cross seeks able-bodied volunteers to aid in evacuating residents tonight and through the morning hours tomorrow." The announcer gave a telephone number and then said, "We repeat the first bulletin: hurricane Ethrelda, with winds up to a hundred miles an hour, is expected to strike the northern Florida coast around noon tomorrow."

I snapped the radio off. Low-lying areas. Despite its limestone bluff on the seaward side, Dolor Island was of no great elevation. But that red brick house, in its almost two centuries of existence, must have withstood many hurricanes, and would withstand this one.

And then I thought of the scrap of blue cloth in my shoulder bag. The storm would strike around noon, the announcer had said. Well, that would leave me the whole morning in which to get to Galton Beach and back.

I left the VW in the empty garage, circled around to the north lawn, and entered the silent house.

Nineteen

Perhaps it was the strain of the funeral. Perhaps it was the humid, oppressive air. Whatever the reason, when my mother returned with the others around five-thirty and climbed to our connecting rooms, her face was white and wan. While they were saying good-by at the cemetery gates, she told me, Dr. Satherly had prescribed that she get a good night's sleep.

·"I asked him to come back to the house for dinner, but he said he didn't feel up to it."

"You don't look up to it, either. Suppose I ask Mrs. Escobar if we can both have dinner up here tonight."

"I'd like that."

I spent a good part of the next hour trying to join my shoulder bag to its strap. After breaking two needles, I gave up. I'd do without it tomorrow. I had just placed the bag back on my bureau when I heard the MG's engine. Looking out, I saw Kevin and Lisa heading for the road down to the gate. Evidently they, too, would be absent from the dinner table tonight.

A few minutes later Mrs. Escobar came in with a large dinner tray, set it on the dressing table, and then, from a closet in the upstairs hall, brought in a small folding table. The funeral, she explained, had been too much for Lorena. She seemed completely unstrung.

"I'm sorry, Mrs. Escobar. And I'm sorry to make extra work for you."

"It does not matter. Mrs. Warren, too, wants dinner in her room, and so I will not have to set the table tonight." She paused. "Will you please fill the bathtub before you go to bed?"

When I looked at her inquiringly, she added, "The storm may arrive earlier than they think it will. If the power plant fails, there will be no running water. I will draw enough water downstairs for drinking and for cooking."

After we had finished dinner, I drew a tubful of water, so as not to disturb Mother later on. Then we sat playing bridge at the folding table. On the transistor radio, tuned low, an announcer talked of the storm, already bearing down on Key West.

My mother said, "I wonder what will become of her?"

"Who?" I asked patiently.

"Amy Warren. She can't go on staying here as a guest, now that Evelyn's dead."

"Sheriff Bixby has taken care of that for the present," I pointed out. "She has to stay."

"But what about afterwards? I don't think she has much money."

"She'll make out."

"The young are so callous."

"Not really. She's saved all her living expenses for

the past six months. And Aunt Evelyn mentioned once that she'd given her several valuable trinkets—jewelry, I guess.

"Before I forget," I added casually. "I'm going over to Galton Beach tomorrow. I need nail polish and a new toothbrush. Want anything?"

"Tomorrow! But, Jenny, the hurricane!"

"Oh, I'll go early enough that there'll be no danger."

"Well, I suppose you can get there and back in half an hour. Could you bring me a few stamps and some cold cream?"

Mother went to bed soon after that. Shortly after I said good night to her, I heard the MG come along the drive and then turn toward the garage. I did not hear them come into the house, but I did hear the closing of Lisa's door, and then Kevin's across the hall. I still sat there, trying to read the last chapter of *Emma*.

But my mother's words about Amy Warren kept getting between me and the printed page. It was true that Amy might be feeling bereft and alone now, and worried about her future. At last I laid the book aside, went down the hall, and tapped softly on her door.

When she opened it, wearing a hair net and an old pink chenille robe, I saw apprehension leap into her little eyes. What was she afraid of? That I was going to suggest she move to Galton Beach pending the end of the sheriff's investigation? Or that I was going to make a fuss about whatever presents Aunt Evelyn had given her?

I said, smiling, "Could I talk to you for a few minutes?"

"Why, of course, dear."

As I entered the room and sat down in the chintz

armchair she offered, I was aware of the odor of sandal-wood. Incense. It seemed as incongruous with this room—its bureau crowded with family photographs, its walls hung with garish oil landscapes she must have brought with her from St. Augustine—as it did with the dumpy little woman who sat on the dressing table bench.

I said, "It's none of my business, of course, so please don't answer unless you want to. But my mother and I were wondering what you plan to do after everything's —I mean, after the sheriff's investigation is over."

My tone must have reassured her, because the hands she had clasped in her lap relaxed slightly. "Oh, go back to St. Augustine. Just this morning I phoned a woman I know there. She says there's a vacancy in her apartment house. Of course, the rent is more than I used to pay."

She hesitated, and then went on, "That's why I'd like to mention something to you. If Evelyn's jewelry is recovered—well, I suppose she left an inventory with her lawyer or someone."

So it was the jewelry that was worrying her. "I imagine so. She never asked me to inventory it."

"Well, you'll find there's a pearl ring and a diamond chip brooch missing. Evelyn gave them to me. I can't prove it, but she did."

Mingled apprehension and defiance in her eyes now. I said, "You don't have to prove it. My aunt told me that she had given you some jewelry."

"Oh, I'm so glad. They're not terribly valuable, but still, it's good to know you have a little something extra against a rainy day."

"Of course it is. Well, I'll let you get to bed now."

She moved with me across the room. I grasped the doorknob and then, on impulse, turned toward her. "Amy, my first night here on the island—"

"Yes, dear?"

"Well, I didn't intend to eavesdrop, but I came to my aunt's room that night to tell her about a trespasser I'd seen. I overheard you and Aunt Evelyn talking."

Her eyes were unreadable now. "How much did you hear?"

Somehow I did not want to mention the chanting. "Enough to know that she thought she had seen a ghost, and she was afraid."

I could see calculation in her eyes now. If she told me about it, might it bring her future benefits?

At last she said, "I think of you as a friend, dear. I hope we'll go on being friends. And now that poor Evelyn is gone—well, I see no reason why you shouldn't know." She paused. "Of course, you already know that Evelyn felt very bitter about your mother's marriage."

I nodded.

"But what Evelyn never told anyone until she told me was that her father wanted to become reconciled to your mother. In fact, he planned to ask her and her husband here for a long visit."

"No, I didn't know that." How much it would have meant to my mother all these years to have known that her father, before he died, had wanted her to come home.

"You can imagine," Amy said, "how Evelyn felt about it."

"Yes." She must have been furious at the thought of her sister and the man she herself had wanted, not only reconciled to my grandfather, and sharing in his will, but sleeping in the same room beneath this roof.

"The night your grandfather had his last heart attack, he and Evelyn had been quarreling about it down in the library. When the attack came, he clutched his chest and gestured for Evelyn to get his heart capsules from the desk."

After a moment I said in a voice that sounded strange and flat even to my own ears, "But she didn't do it."

"No, she just walked out of the library. About fifteen minutes later this Polish maid they had then came into the library to turn off the lights for the night. She found Mr. Dunway dead.

"If I hadn't known Evelyn was truly remorseful," Amy went on, "I would not have continued to be her friend after she told me about what she had done. But she had been remorseful for years. In fact, after her father's death, she isolated herself on this island."

Remorseful? Or afraid that the Polish servant—who no doubt was promptly dismissed, with a generous bonus—had overheard that final quarrel, and might circulate rumors about her?

"Anyway," Amy said, "one night about a week before she and I became acquainted in that beauty parlor, Evelyn climbed the stairs and looked down the hall toward her room. Her father was standing there, outside her door. After a second or two, he disappeared."

I said, feeling sick, "Promise me one thing."

"Of course, dear."

"Don't tell this story to anyone else. I don't want there to be even a chance that my mother will ever know how my grandfather died."

"Of course I promise. And I do hope you know that

I realize what a terrible thing it was that Evelyn did. But after all, I couldn't undo it, could I? And so I gave her my friendship and came here to protect her, and at the same time persuade her father's poor, restless spirit that she had already paid with many lonely, remorseful years for her sin against him."

I felt an impulse to ask, "Do you really believe that she saw my grandfather standing outside her door? And about that protection. Do you believe you have special powers? Or are you an out-and-out fraud?"

But I didn't ask, and not just because of a reluctance to be rude. I remembered oak leaves rattling in a sudden wind. I remembered the fury that had leaped into the little gray eyes at dinner that first night when Kevin baited her. And, quite frankly, I was afraid to have her look at me like that.

I said, "Well, please remember not to tell anyone else about this."

"My dear girl, my lips are sealed. Believe me."

"Good night," I said, and walked down the hall to my own room.

The sense of oppression I felt had nothing to do with grief. My grandfather had died three years before I was born. What's more, I realized that probably he would have died even if Aunt Evelyn had given him his medicine. After all, he'd had three previous heart attacks. No, what weighed upon me was the thought of her turning her back upon the stricken man and walking from the room.

No use in trying to read. I had better get to bed.

I was about to unzip my dress when the phone a few feet from my door rang. Quickly, lest my mother be disturbed, I moved out into the hall and picked up the handset. A man's voice asked, through a loud crackling on the line, "Is Shaughnessy around?"

"Why, yes." I heard a door open. "Here he is now." I turned. "It's for you."

As Kevin moved toward me, a strained smile on his face, he said, "Hope it didn't wake the help."

"I don't think so. I caught it before the second ring."

He took the phone from my hand, and I went into my room and closed the door. I heard him say in a sharp voice, "What news?" His voice sank to a murmur after that, but now and then, as I undressed, he spoke loudly enough that I heard a phrase or two. Once he said sharply, "I can't, not tonight." Then, more heatedly: "You'll just have to take my decision on it, that's all."

I was in my nightgown when I heard a soft tap on the door panel. Belting my robe around me, I crossed the room and opened the door.

"Bad news," Kevin said. "I'll have to go to St. Augustine early in the morning, hurricane or no hurricane. My aunt's pretty sick. That was her husband on the phone. Will you tell the others where I've gone? I'll try to get back before the storm hits. If the power goes out, I'll see if I can jerry-rig something."

"I'll tell them. And I'm sorry about your aunt."

"Well, maybe she'll be better by the time I get there. 'Night."

Good night," I said, and closed the door. Something strange about that call. Perhaps it was static caused by the approaching storm, but the caller had sounded much farther away than St. Augustine. And then there was the tone of Kevin's voice. He had not sounded like someone discussing a seriously ill relative. What was more, I could see no reason why he hadn't driven over there tonight.

And come to think of it, what sort of man referred to his nephew by his last name?

Then I tried to dismiss the thought of Kevin, as well as the thought of my aunt and the grandfather I had never known, both of them dead now. I had an immediate concern of my own—that very much alive sheriff over in Galton Beach. Suppression of evidence for a few hours might be forgivable. But by tomorrow morning I would have had that scrap of cloth in my possession for more than three days.

I set the alarm for seven-thirty. Then I got into bed, turned off the light, and lay awake for perhaps half an hour, aware of the brooding silence, before I fell asleep.

Twenty

Minutes before the alarm was due to go off, I awoke to gray light and to gentle rain pattering against the windows. I dressed quickly and quietly in white duck pants, a striped jersey, and my hooded plaid raincoat. I started to pick up my shoulder bag, and then remembered its useless strap. Better to do without a bag. I put the envelope containing the torn scrap into my raincoat pocket, and thrust my billfold and car keys in after it.

I had intended to leave the house immediately, but as I neared the foot of the stairs, the smell of hot coffee assailed my nostrils. Perhaps it would be wiser not to face an enraged sheriff on an empty stomach. In the deserted dining room, I served myself a hasty but adequate breakfast of orange juice and scrambled eggs. Then I went out through the softly falling rain to the garage.

Only the Lincoln and my bug stood there. Apparently Kevin had already set out for St. Augustine. I drove the VW through the misty gray light down to the locked gate. Harley, in jeans and in a shirt of black-and-white checked cotton, came out of the little cottage. Feeling guilty, I recognized the shirt as one of those I'd seen folded in his bureau drawer. And then, as I remembered the seashell that lay between the two picture frames, my happiness overcame my guilt.

"Good morning, Cerberus," I said. "Open up thy gates."

His voice was soft. "Good morning." Then, in a firm tone: "Just where do you think you're going?"

"Galton Beach. I need a few things. And I should get back in plenty of time. After all, Kevin said he was going clear to St. Augustine and back."

"Kevin had to. He needs parts for a new generator in case the power goes out. But all right. Hurry back, though. Daytona is already catching hell." He moved to the gate and unlocked the padlock.

No mention of Kevin's aunt. Hadn't Kevin told him about that? Harley came back to the VW and said, "If you run into my dopey sister over there, tell her to get back here."

"She went to Galton Beach?"

"Bicycled over. Said she wanted to see the town battening down for the hurricane. So bring her back, huh? The gate will be open."

"You won't be here?"

"No. The Red Cross needs men to evacuate people from Beal and Black Turtle Islands. They're flat as a pancake, you know. I'm going to meet a power boat over at the dock in half an hour."

"Quite an exodus," I said. "Like rats leaving the ship."

He smiled. "Except that Dolor Island won't sink, no

181

matter how much water we ship. Now get your gum-drops or whatever, and hurry back."

I drove along the causeway, across gray water dimpled with rain that fell harder now. As I turned onto the main street of Galton Beach, I saw the bartender who had served beer to Harley and me a few days before. He was out on the sidewalk hammering boards across his plate glass window. The dirty window of Barney's Quick Lunch opposite was still unprotected. Perhaps Barney hoped it would shatter, thus enabling him to get from his insurance company a new one that wouldn't need washing.

No loungers on the hotel steps today. But a group of loud-talking, gesticulating men had gathered on the sagging veranda. I thought of the excitement which grips some people at the approach of a storm—an excitement which can take the form of murderous rage or of a sometimes-fatal euphoria which, especially if heightened by alcohol, can keep its victims from seeking shelter.

The window of the sheriff's office, next to the abandoned movie theater, was still unprotected, although folded steel shutters had been affixed at either end. Through the glass I could see Sheriff Bixby talking into a telephone.

Overwhelmed by cowardice, I drove on. A few minutes' delay would not matter. I would get my mother's cold cream and stamps first, and then call on the sheriff.

As I approached the drugstore, a truck with the words *St. Augustine Sun-Courier* painted on its side pulled away from the curb. I parked, and then climbed two steps to the door beside a boarded-up display window. A bicycle leaned against the boards. Lisa's?

Yes, she sat at the soda fountain, wearing chinos and a T-shirt, hair gleaming beneath the fluorescent light. She held a bottle of Dr. Pepper in her hand. As I walked toward her, she turned to look at me.

"Hello, Lisa." She nodded. I went on, "Harley's worried about you. He wants you to come back."

"Harley's an old granny. I like hurricanes."

Irritated with her for making me sound stuffy, I said, "You won't like it if you and your bike get washed off the causeway."

"Who's going to get washed off? I figure I've got another hour, at least."

"Maybe. But don't cut it too fine."

I put coins in the stamp machine, and then moved to the store's one counter. A gray-haired woman took cold cream down from a shelf, all the time talking about the storm, and put it in a paper bag. I started toward the door, and then stopped beside a metal rack which held copies of the St. Augustine paper. The banner line read: *Ethrelda Bearing Down on Florida Coast.* I dropped a dime in the slot and took a paper from the rack. Aware that I was postponing that moment when I would walk into Sheriff Bixby's office, I skimmed through the first paragraphs of the lead story, and then turned the paper over to read below the center fold.

Side by side, two photographs of the same swarthy-complexioned man seemed to leap up at me. The full-face photo showed expressionless dark eyes under straight-across brows, and a thin mouth. The profile picture showed me what I had seen, illuminated by a cigarette lighter's flare, my first night on Dolor Island —a receding hairline, hawk nose, and a scar that ran from temple to chin. I did not need the barely legible

183

numbers at the bottom of each photograph to tell me that they came from police files.

My eyes dropped to the headline beneath the pictures: "Alleged Leader of International Narcotics Ring Arrested in Manhattan." Swiftly I skimmed through the story. "Emile Revelle, 33, Algerian-born Frenchman—long sought as an organizer of wartime dope traffic in Indonesia—wanted by police of France and Turkey—means of entry into the United States still unknown."

My gaze went back to the photos—photos of a man who, for profit, had sown degradation, torment, and death in both hemispheres of the world. No wonder I had felt sure, as I looked through the screen of leaves that night, that I stood only a few feet from some monstrous evil.

Lisa spoke, so close to me that I gave a start. "What's the *matter* with you?"

"That man," I said, and handed her the paper.

She frowned down at the pictures. "Some big shot pusher caught. So what?"

"He's the man I saw on the beach path the first night I was down here."

She stared at me. "You're sure?"

"I'm positive."

She looked at me silently for another few seconds, and then said in a low, shaking voice, "That bastard. That lying bastard."

I said, bewildered, "But you didn't sound as if you knew—"

"Oh, I don't mean *him!*" She struck the paper with the back of her hand. "I mean Kevin. He made a fool of me, the lying, filthy—"

Her face had twisted now, and she was crying. Despite the violence of her language, she looked very young, like a little girl who had just learned that her best friend stole her dolly.

"Lisa, what—"

"Kevin made a sucker of me, and a sucker of Harley." She flung the paper from her and bolted out into the rain.

I stood there, turning cold all over. Harley. What did Harley have to do with a narcotics dealer? Then, unmindful of the lady proprietor moving toward me, I hurried out the door. Lisa, long hair plastered to her back by the driving rain, was already pedaling down the street. I got into the VW, inserted the key with shaking fingers, and drove after her. Slowing beside her, I cried, "Lisa, get in the car."

She gave me a blind, furious look, and went on pedaling. "Damn it!" I yelled. "Get in the car."

She stopped. There was strong wind now, as well as much heavier rain. The bike twisted in her hands as she lifted it toward the luggage rack, and the front wheel banged against the car's top. She shoved the bike into place and then got in beside me, using both hands to close the door against a gust of wind that threatened to tear it from its hinges. Wavering light through the rain-drenched windshield, combined with the angry tears still flowing down her face, made her look like someone glimpsed beneath shallow water.

I put the car in gear and moved on down the street. "What's this about you and Harley being suckers?"

"He told us they were deserters, and we believed him."

"They?"

"The men he's hidden on the island one time or another, and then smuggled over to the mainland. I thought there'd been three, so far, but who knows with a liar like that?"

I persisted, "Army deserters?"

"Guys who'd blown their stacks in Vietnam and gone awol. They had no other way of getting back into the country, Kevin said."

"And Harley knew about this?"

"Sure. He'd have been a cinch to find out, so Kevin told him. Harley wouldn't have anything to do with it. He's pretty much of a straight, you know. But at the same time, he didn't want to blow the whistle on Kevin."

She paused, and then said bitterly, "You can imagine how Kevin put it to him. Here were these poor damn grunts who'd been driven out of their skulls. Not clean, well-fed pilots like Harley, mind you, but guys who'd had it so tough they'd cracked up and gone over the hill. And here was noble Kevin, risking Leavenworth to help get them back to home and Mother. And all for nothing.

"Nothing!" she repeated furiously. "Why, I'll bet he's got hundreds of thousands stashed away to his credit somewhere, maybe in some Hongkong bank."

We were crossing the causeway now, over water that seethed with whitecaps. Gusts of wind slammed against the little car, rocking it. I said dazedly, "He went to St. Augustine this morning."

"St. Augustine! What do you bet he caught some plane that took off ahead of the storm? He's probably in New York now, getting aboard a plane for Amsterdam or Paris or someplace."

I was silent, remembering that phone call of the night before. Someone had warned him that Emile Revelle had been arrested and might talk, and so it would be best to leave the island right away. I could see why he had not. Even if he had provided himself with a key to the gate padlock, Harley might have heard him and come out. And no story about a sick aunt would have served to explain his hasty, middle-of-the-night departure. Kevin probably had no aunt, sick or well, in St. Augustine, and Harley probably knew it.

"Of course," Lisa said, "if he wasn't able to get a plane in St. Augustine, he might come back here to try to hole up for a few more days. He's just conceited enough to think that he could con us with some story about how that guy had taken him in, too."

We drove through the open gate, across the clearing which surrounded the cottage, and onto the road that led through the pines. Here the car no longer rocked. But above and around us there was a continuous roar, as if we moved through a wind tunnel. I pitched my voice below the sound. "Where did Kevin hide those men?"

Not in the caretaker's cottage. Pray God, not the cottage.

She had stopped crying now. Her voice was sullen. "Why do you want to know?"

"Because I'm concerned about Harley."

She gave me a bitter little smile. "I thought that's how it was. Well, lots of luck. Better luck than I had with Kevin, anyway."

"Where did he hide those men? Or don't you know?"

"Oh, I know. I was awake one night when one of them came off a motor launch onto the dock. The guy had bribed the captain of a Greek freighter, Kevin told me afterward, and crossed over from Europe in the hold. Greek freighter! I'll bet it was some Marseilles mobster's hundred-foot yacht.

"But anyway," she went on, "I followed him and Kevin after he landed, so I know. But I don't think I'll tell you. If I weren't so goddamned mad, I wouldn't have told you this much."

I did not answer. We emerged from the pine-sheltered road into the full force of the torrential rain, and into wind that slammed like a giant fist into the little car and peppered its glass with driveway gravel. I did not try to speak again until we had driven into the garage and stopped beside the Lincoln.

"Lisa, did Kevin kill my aunt?"

After a moment she answered sullenly, "He said not. But how can you tell with someone like that?"

"If he did it, do you think it was for her jewelry?"

"Jewelry! What does he need jewelry for, with all the money he must have stashed away?"

"Why, then? Because he hated her?"

She threw me a contemptuous look. "You didn't read him at all, did you? Kevin's a real cool head. He wouldn't risk ruining his little setup here, no matter how much he hated her."

"Could he have had some other reason?"

She said broodingly, "Oh, I suppose so. If he thought she had found out and was just sitting back, waiting to pounce . . . She might have done that, you know."

"She might have. Lisa, where did Kevin hide those men?"

She said with sudden fury, "I'm sick of your questions. Stop hassling me."

188

She got out, slammed the door, and ran from the garage. By the time I got to the doorway, she was running through the uproar of wind and rain toward the eastern side of the house and the stairs leading up to the balcony.

I could see Mrs. Escobar beyond the windows of the lighted kitchen. Head bent, I ran across the rear lawn. Just before I reached the back door, she opened it and then closed it behind me.

She made no comment upon Lisa's wild dash toward the corner of the house. "You look half drowned," she said.

I looked at the water dripping from my raincoat onto the linoleum. "I'm sorry to mess up your floor."

"That's all right." She paused. "The phone's dead, and probably the power will go out too, and so I've been getting these lamps ready." She nodded toward a row of oil lamps that stood on the Formica-topped table. "Would you mind carrying two of them upstairs? There's so much to do down here."

"Of course not."

Carrying the lamps, and with the storm's surflike roar in my ears, I moved through halls already plunged into twilight gloom and up the curving stairs.

Twenty-One

Around ten that night, an awesome thing happened. As if a huge hand somewhere in the universe had pulled a switch, the storm ceased. The wind died, and the rain dwindled to a light patter, then to silence. Standing at the window of my dimly lit room, I watched with incredulity while a rent widened in the clouds, and blue-white Vega and her sister stars shone against the black sky.

The island was in the eye of the storm, that low-pressure area around which the winds swirled. Sometime soon—in half an hour, an hour, maybe more—the wind and the rain would strike again, this time from the opposite direction. In the meantime, this interval of peace.

But for many hours the island had been in the grip of a fury so relentless that sometimes I had expected the house to topple or engulfing seas to rush in on us. The gusts of wind slamming the VW as Lisa and I drove back from Galton Beach had been only a prelude. By noon the power had gone off, the day was almost as dark as at an hour past sunset, and the wind made a continuous roar, sometimes interspersed with shrieking sounds, like the tearing of some vast garment of silk, and rumblings as of some mile-long freight train. Soon there was no front lawn, only a shallow lake, dully gleaming in the half darkness, its surface strewn with branches ripped from trees. And always there was the noise—continuous, maddening, making speech and even thought almost impossible.

There was no solitary dining that night. As if needing the comfort of each other's presence, we all gathered in the dining room for cold meat and salad. Mrs. Escobar and Lorena, too, I noticed, were in the room a great deal of the time, not only serving the food, but renewing the candles that burned on the long table and the buffet, and sopping up water that penetrated around the window frames to trickle down onto the floor.

We had given up trying to talk. Amy and Mother and Lisa and I sat silently at the table. Mrs. Escobar and Lorena moved silently about their tasks. The candlelight, wavering in the air currents that penetrated even this solid house, did strange and unpleasant things to faces. In the play of light and shadow, Amy's face and even my mother's gentle one took on a harsh, witchlike aspect. Sometimes that uncertain light, playing over Lisa's brooding face and almost white hair, made her look hollow-eyed and baleful, like something out of a Norse legend of beautiful but demonic spirits. Mrs. Escobar's calm features, as she moved about the room, seemed to shift and waver, and the nervous smile on Lorena's swarthy face, even darker in the candlelight, took on the aspect of a grimace.

Six women. And a murderer among us?

It was a thought I did not welcome, but in the wavering light of that room, with the howling of a thousand devils outside, it seemed inescapable. Kevin, Lisa had said in effect, would not kill without a good reason, and to him dislike or even hatred of my aunt, or the money he could obtain for her jewelry, would not be a sufficiently good reason. But the jewelry might have been sufficient reason for light-fingered Lisa, or even for Amy, who had been dependent upon a rich woman's whim as to whether she went on living in this luxurious house or returned to some cramped room or apartment in St. Augustine. Perhaps she had decided that she needed more jewelry than just a pearl ring and a diamond chip brooch to shield her against a rainy day. And when it came to hatred as a possible reason for murder . . . I looked at Mrs. Escobar and Lorena over by the window, mopping up with woolen cloths and wringing them out into a bucket, and wondered how often they thought of the child who had been one woman's son, the other's grandnephew.

No, it would be unbearable during the long hours ahead to think that Aunt Evelyn's killer still moved through this storm-locked house. The one who had wielded that candlestick must be somewhere out there beyond this drenched and wind-tormented island.

Was Harley still working with the rescue crew? No, by this time, with high seas smashing on beaches and the air full of flying missiles, the rescue crews must have had to leave any who had tarried on low ground to their fates. He was in shelter someplace, waiting for the end of the storm. As for Kevin, who could say whether he was in St. Augustine, or New York, or on a plane flying above the dark Atlantic?

We went to our rooms after dinner. For a while my mother and I sat in her room, dimly lighted by an old oil lamp with red roses painted on its china base. Then my mother, looking apologetic, crossed to the bureau, opened a drawer, and held out a vial of yellow capsules to me. Sleeping pills. I nodded. A pill might send her off to sleep despite that uproar outside. I kissed her cheek and went into my own room.

That had been a little more than an hour ago. And now this silence. During the past hours, a universe in tumult had begun to seem the norm, so that now it was this silence that seemed unnatural.

But the silence was not complete. I heard a popping sound somewhere below, followed by the tinkle of glass. Because of the abrupt drop in air pressure, a window had burst outward.

Another sound. A soft tap on my door.

By the time I opened it, Lisa had retreated to the head of the stairs. She turned, long hair gleaming in the dim light from the oil lamp on the hall table, and beckoned to me. I closed the door quietly and walked toward her.

She said in a sullen voice, "I've changed my mind. I'll show you where he hid those men."

I said, after a startled moment, "Why?"

"Don't waste time asking questions. That damned wind will be back, you know. Now do you want to see, or don't you?"

I nodded. Best not to irritate her, lest she change her mind again. "Are we going outside?"

"Yes. Better wear boots and a raincoat. It'll be plenty

wet under the trees."

I felt a stab of dread. The trees. Did she mean the pines along the road that led down to the cottage?

"Don't stand there," she said. "Hurry."

I went back to my room, swiftly donned my raincoat, and pulled on the only boots I had, ankle-length ones of transparent plastic, over my flat-soled sandals. I left the room and moved toward her.

"We'll go through my room," she said, "onto the balcony."

The oil lamp on the apple-green dressing table in her room gave me a brief glimpse of pinup photos on the wall—Steve McQueen and Mick Jagger and Michael Caine—and of a long-legged cloth doll sprawled on a white organdy bedspread. Fleetingly I wondered at the girlishness. But then, why shouldn't her room be girlish? She was eighteen, although sometimes she seemed much older than that, and sometimes younger.

We stepped out onto the balcony's wet tiled floor. I glanced to my left, toward that corner room Aunt Evelyn had occupied. The limb of the live oak, unbroken, still stretched toward the railing, but the white wicker chair and the matching table that had toppled over that night were gone. Perhaps Mrs. Escobar had removed them as a precaution. Or perhaps the wind had whirled them away.

I followed her through the strange silence along the balcony and down the outside staircase. On the square of cement at the foot stood an unlit lantern, with a coil of rope beside it. She must have taken them, I realized, from the garage. "Don't talk," she whispered.

I nodded. The dimly lighted windows of Mrs. Escobar's and Lorena's quarters were only a few feet away.

"Take these." She thrust what felt like a small box of matches into my hand, slung the coil of rope over her shoulder, and picked up the lantern.

To my dizzying relief, she did not turn toward the front of the house and the drive. Instead I followed her across the sopping wilderness of the east lawn, strewn with large branches that I could avoid, and small ones that caught at the legs of my white ducks. Throwing a glance upward, I saw that more stars shone between wisps of hurrying clouds.

We entered the wide graveled path that led to the beach. About ten yards along it, she stopped. "We can talk now. Give me the matches."

She lit the lantern. Its yellow glow showed me a face both bitter and determined. She said, giving the matches back to me, "Hold onto them. This lantern may go out. There's something wrong with the damned wick."

We walked side by side now. I could hear the steady drip of moisture from the trees, mingled with the roar of surf on the island's seaward side. I said, "Why did you change your mind?"

She burst out after a moment's brooding silence, "Because I'm the only one besides Kevin who knows. I want someone else to know, just in case."

"Where he kept those men?"

"Yes!" Her voice was heavy with sarcasm. "Where he kept those poor, mind-blown GI's of his."

"Doesn't Harley know?"

"Harley! He wanted to know as little about it as possible. Besides, I decided long ago that the less you tell old Harley, the better off you are."

Sure, I thought. Worry him half to death. Let him

suffer a hell of humiliation to protect you from what was coming to you. But don't tell the old straight anything.

I said, "But why are you letting me know?"

"I told you. I'd tell Harley now if he was here, but he isn't. And I think Kevin may come back. He may be on his way back now."

I had a chilly vision of the MG driving over the causeway, through the open gate. "But why would he come back? This morning you said he'd probably try to leave the country."

"I know. But I got to thinking about it at dinner. Maybe there's a pound or so of hard stuff stashed away where he kept those men."

So that was what she had been thinking about while the wavering candlelight turned her into some baleful goddess out of a Norse legend.

"Maybe he was in too much of a panic to take it with him," she went on. "But if he's cooled off now—well, a few hundred thousand dollars' worth of H would be worth coming back for, wouldn't it?" Her voice went flat. "And worth shutting me up for, too."

I repeated slowly, "Shutting you up?"

"Yes! Don't you see? I'm the only one who knows where his little hideaway is. That's why I want you to know, too."

I halted. I said, feeling cold ripples down my spine, "Lisa, are you trying to tell me that you're afraid Kevin will come back here and kill you?"

She, too, stopped. In the lantern's upward striking light her bitter face looked years older than her actual age. "Of course he would, if he decided he had to, and that he could get away with it."

"Lisa, let's go back to the house."

She said angrily, "You can't chicken out, not now."

"If he's that dangerous, and if he's on his way back here—"

"I meant maybe he was coming back as far as Galton Beach! He can't get across the causeway now. It must be under water. But maybe he'll get back here as soon as he can. And don't tell me I'll be safe as soon as Harley gets back. Harley may be out with the rescue crews for a couple of days after the storm's over, getting people back into their houses. And don't tell me I can go over and tell the sheriff tomorrow. Kevin may not give me the chance!"

She paused, and then said passionately, "You've got to do this for me. If anything happens to me—well, I don't want him to get away with it. I want you to be able to tell the police the whole thing, even," she said bitterly, "where they can find his little treasure trove, if he's left one there. Now come *on!*"

There had been something childishly, almost tearfully urgent about those last words. I looked at her flushed face. Would a man really kill a girl like that? Men did. Girls who learned too much about the wrong kind of men sometimes died violently, even girls as young and beautiful as Lisa.

Not speaking, I fell into step beside her.

She turned onto the path leading to the pavilion. Here where the tree branches met overhead, dripping moisture made a steady patter on my raincoat hood, and fell in silvery, elongated drops through the lantern's glow. The pavilion? How could he have kept anyone hidden in that open-sided structure?

I followed her up the two low steps. Not only rain

197

water but small branches had blown in between the pillars, littering the square flagstones. As she moved, lantern light washed over the little figure, still standing with cupped hands in the shallow basin, and dimly illuminated the rows of lion heads, each with a ring in its mouth, attached to the pillars on the pavilion's eastern side.

She set down the lantern near the basin and slid the coil of rope from her shoulder. I asked, "What are you doing?"

Busy knotting one end of the rope around the cherub's neck, she did not answer. Bending, she picked up the coil of rope, carried it to the nearest pillar, and threaded the other rope end through the ring dangling from a lion's mouth. It was not until then that she said, "I have to do it this way because the power is out."

I said, "Power? I don't—"

"Kevin ran a buried cable from the power house back here. All you have to do is this." She jabbed her forefinger viciously inside the lion's mouth. "But with the power out . . ."

As she moved to the next pillar and began to thread the rope through the ring, I suddenly understood.

Twelve-year-old Kevin, that afternoon when, with a garden hose, he had made the fountain work. There had been chips of mortar lying around the basin, and a coil of rope near one of the pillars. "What's all that for?" I asked. And he had answered, "Nothing. I was just fooling around."

She ran the rope through still a third ring, pulled it tant. "Don't just stand there," she said. "Help me. Stand in front of me."

Dazedly obedient, I moved over the littered floor and

grasped the rope.

"Now pull."

We both pulled. The far edge of the flagstone to which the little fountain was attached lifted two inches above the floor, three inches. A door, I thought, leading to some hidden place below ground. How long, I wondered, with a weird detachment, had that subterranean place been there? And then I realized that it must be older than this pavilion. In fact, the chief purpose of this concrete structure, and of the little fountain, must have been to conceal what lay below.

I could feel the rope cutting into my palms, and hear my own labored breath, and Lisa's. For a moment the cherub seemed to hang there, head pointed at an angle toward the pavilion's roof. "Now!" Lisa said. I gathered all my strength and pulled. The cherub's head angled another inch or so toward us, seemed to hesitate, and then, as the flagstone rose to stand at right angles to the floor, the top of the little bronze head pointed straight at us.

Lisa said, "You can drop it."

I dropped the rope. Fleetingly I wondered if Kevin, that long-ago day, had been able to raise that trap door more than an inch or two. Probably not. But even one inch would have been enough to bring all his stubborn curiosity into play, and his innate mechanical talent.

Lisa was moving toward the trap door. I followed. Lifting the lantern, she held it so that I could see the glitter of steel hinges where once there must have been rusted iron. From the opposite side of the opening, crude stone steps angled down through a timbered and whitewashed shaft.

"Kevin told me that when he first found this place

the old timbers had collapsed, and the bottom steps were buried in sand. It took him a whole year, working at night, to get the sand out. And he wasn't able to finish the timbering until he got back from Vietnam."

A whole year. I thought of the young boy, stubbornly defiant of the woman who controlled his mother's destiny and his, slipping through the woods at night to this pavilion. And I thought of the adult Kevin, a corrupt and able associate of men who would never pass an immigration inspector, returning to this island to cash in on his boyhood discovery.

Still holding the lantern, Lisa started down the timeworn steps. It is only with reluctance that I enter any underground place, even a cellar. I hesitated, and then followed, one hand trailing along the timbered wall for support. I could hear a hollow, sustained roar now. It grew louder as I descended.

At the bottom of the steps another, horizontal shaft led away at right angles. I followed Lisa for about thirty feet along its timbered length. The hollow quality of that sustained sound was more pronounced now. It was almost like being inside a huge kettledrum. Then we stepped through a rough stone archway, and I saw that we were indeed inside a kind of drum, a cavern hewn out of limestone. And the stormy sea, hurling its waves up the beach to pound against the limestone bluff, was the mighty drummer.

Just inside the archway was a stainless steel table holding an alcohol stove and an acetylene lantern, larger and obviously much newer than the battered one Lisa carried. She set the old lantern on the table. I looked at the stove for a moment, and then at the steel shelf above it, affixed to the rock wall. The shelf held canned goods and a bottle of cognac, almost full. Then

I took a step or two forward, and stood looking around me.

The cavern, I saw, was roughly circular, with pebbly sand as its floor, and with walls that curved upward to form a low roof. Close to the curving wall was a narrow metal bed, neatly made up with khaki blankets and a turned-back top sheet. Beside the bed was a metal stand holding an ashtray filled with cigarette stubs, and a magazine. Even from several feet away I could read its title—*Lui,* the French version of *Playboy.* Near the foot of the bed was a steel door, about two and a half feet square, set in the limestone wall perhaps three feet above the sandy floor. A hasp, with a metal bolt through it, held the door shut.

Lisa said in a tone of brooding satisfaction, "Well, now you know."

I did not answer. I was staring at the steel door. Lisa said, "There was a piece of rusty old iron there before Kevin put in the stainless steel."

I nodded, remembering a young boy who had removed fragments of eroded limestone from the rear wall of that outer cave, and thrust his hand through the small opening he had made and exclaimed excitedly, "It feels like iron."

Well, he had found no treasure chest. But in a sense he had found pirates' gold. Modern pirates who preyed, not on merchant ships and their crews, but on wretched men and women all over the earth. I looked at the end of a metal box, barely visible beneath the foot of the bed. A strongbox? And if so, was it empty now, or did it hold money, or packets of deadly white powder?

And then, near the bed's steel leg, I saw something that had escaped my attention until then. On the sandy floor lay a few links of rusting chain, still bolted to the wall. Feeling sick, I turned around. Along the wall curving away from the cave's entrance were more bolts and rusty chains, one with a leg iron still attached. I imagined them, those moaning men and women and children from across the ocean, not knowing what lay ahead, knowing only that they were shackled down here in darkness.

Why had Kevin left those chains there? And then I realized that there was no reason why he should not have. A man who profited by one form of slavery would not turn squeamish over reminders of a more ancient sort.

Lisa said, "Oh, hell! There goes the lantern. Give me the matches."

Eyes fixed anxiously on the smoking, guttering lantern wick, I plunged my hand into my raincoat pocket.

"Hurry! I want to get the other lantern lit. My God, don't tell me you've lost the matches!"

Shaken by the thought of this underground place plunged into darkness, I thrust my hand into my other pocket. Wasn't the box there either? Hand closing around the pocket's entire contents, I brought it out. Yes, there was the box of matches, thank God, and my billfold and car keys, and the remains of a sodden white envelope, clinging to a bit of blue-and-white cloth.

I raised my eyes to look at Lisa. She was staring at the objects in my hand, recognition in her eyes. Then she looked at my face. And after a moment, because of the look that came over her face—the full mouth grimly compressed, the eyes narrowed—I knew with a leap of terror that my own face must have said to her, "So it was you."

Twenty-Two

She picked up the box of matches from my palm. "I hope they're not too wet," she said, and turned to light the acetylene lantern. Swiftly I thrust the other objects in my hand back into my pocket. For perhaps half a minute, while she struck several matches, succeeded in lighting one, and held it to the wick of the shiny new lantern, I was able to tell myself that perhaps I had imagined that silent dialogue between us.

But when she turned back to me, smiling in the stronger light that now filled the cavern, I knew I had imagined nothing.

"So you found it. I wondered who did. Did you show it to the sheriff? No, of course you haven't yet, or he'd have kept it."

I looked at her standing there between me and the entrance to the horizontal shaft, a girl six inches taller than I and perhaps twenty pounds heavier, with muscles hardened by all-year-around swimming and water skiing. I said, aware of the hollow thunder of the sea, aware of that rusty old lantern guttering out, "I don't know what you're talking about."

"Oh, yes you do. But anyway, I buried that torn shirt and the white shorts I wore that night. People could dig for a month without finding them." She paused, and then asked, "Did you have any idea it was me?"

I looked up at her looming over me, pale hair gleaming in the acetylene glow. Try to be matter-of-fact, I warned myself. Above all, don't let her see how frightened you are. After all, she was only eighteen. Perhaps, if I found the right words . . .

"Oh, I thought it might be you. But there were others who had reason to—"

"There sure were." She laughed, and I realized that I had never heard her laugh until then. It was a high, rippling sound, almost like the laughter of a young child. "But I had the best reason of all."

I said casually, hoping she did not see the pounding pulse in the hollow of my throat, "You mean her jewelry?"

"You heard about that bracelet, huh? Oh, sure, I like jewelry. But the jewelry I took from her safe that night was just sort of a bonus. It was the island I wanted."

When I did not answer, she said, "Don't you see? Now that I've torn up that will, Harley gets the island. I can live here all my life."

I stretched my lips into a smile. "I see."

She leaned back against the table and folded her arms across her T-shirt. "I'd thought it was all settled when Harley married her. And then I heard the old bitch telling you that she'd cut Harley off with five thousand."

I said, still with that rigid smile, "So you were the

one who knocked over the table with the ashtray on it. I thought it was a white cat."

"It was the cat that made me do it. I'd just started back to my room when that damned cat began scrambling around on that oak limb. It startled me so much I bumped into the table. But anyway, from that night on I knew I was going to have to kill her and get that will. All I had to do was to wait for the right time."

The right time. A night when my mother had quarreled violently with Aunt Evelyn. Beneath my shock and fear, anger stirred.

"I've always wanted this island, ever since the first time my father brought me here. I was about six then. The only thing wrong with it is that there's no surfing. But then, there really isn't any all along this coast. Australia, that's where the good surfing is. I'm going to go there someday."

She looked at me, smiling. "I'll bet you wish you'd never come to this island." Her smile died. She said coldly, "Well, I tried to make you go. How did you like finding a tarantula in your size-five bootsy-wootsy?"

It came to me then, a way I might distract her thoughts from myself. I said, "But you did that because of Kevin, didn't you? You had the completely wrong idea that he might be interested in me."

"Kevin!" she said bitterly. "Yes, I was afraid you might take him away from me. And all the time he was lying to me, probably laughing at me."

She stared broodingly past my shoulder. "I'd have done anything for Kevin. Why, I even poisoned the dogs for him, and I like dogs, even Dobermans. But Kevin was worried. He said he was expecting another of his awols"—her mouth twisted—"and the dogs might make things tougher for him. So I mixed cock-roach powder with hamburger, and fed it to them. I didn't even tell him about it until after I'd done it. I wanted to make it—like a present to him."

Her brooding eyes still looked past my shoulder. I stood there, listening to the sea's hollow roar. Should I try to dart past her and run along the tunnel and up those stone steps? No, even if I evaded the long arm she would put out, she would run after me and easily over-take me, and I would find I had succeeded only in arousing her murderous rage.

She put her head to one side with a listening air. "Can you hear it?"

"What?"

"The wind. It's starting up again." Then, to my in-credulous and overwhelming relief, she said, "We'd bet-ter go before it gets really strong." She reached for the acetylene lantern. "Well, get moving," she said impa-tiently.

I started toward the tunnel entrance. From the cor-ner of my eye I saw her hand transfer itself from the acet-ylene lantern to the unlighted one, and I tried to throw up my arms to protect my head, but I wasn't fast enough. I felt blinding pain, and then, for a timeless interval, nothing at all.

Twenty-Three

I awoke to throbbing pain. For a few blessed moments, despite the pitch-blackness, and the grit of sand beneath my cheek, and that roaring sound, I did not know where I was.

And then I did know. I was underground, in a place of eternal night. I felt it then, the smothering weight of that most primitive of terrors, the terror of being buried alive.

Stand up, I told myself. Try to get out of here.

My groping hand found the table's steel leg, then its edge. I pulled myself to my feet and stood there, bent over, drawing air deep into my lungs to try to rid myself of that smothering sensation. Despite the blackness, I had to find the tunnel and the stairs.

Letting go of the table, hoping I wouldn't fall, I moved to my left and stretched my arms out in front of me. Two steps forward, three. I stretched my arms to either side of me, felt the tunnel's timbered walls, and moved, staggering, over down-sloping earth. I did not know I had reached the stone stairs until my foot struck the side of the bottom step, pitching me forward. Only my palms, striking against the far wall of the vertical shaft, saved me from falling.

Straightening, I moved a little to my left, took a forward step, and then turned. I knew that now I must be standing at the foot of the stairs. I looked up.

She heard the returning wind, Lisa had said. And she must have heard it, or thought she did. Otherwise she would have delayed long enough to use the lantern as effectively as she had used that candlestick. It seemed to me that I could hear the wind too, a thin howling that rose above the dull roar from the cavern. But no air current stirred the inky blackness down here, and no rain fell on my upturned face.

The trap door was closed.

I felt the full weight of it again, that smothering terror. Breathing raggedly, holding onto the shaft's timbered wall, I climbed several steps, and then raised my arms. My palms flattened themselves against cold stone. I pushed with all my might, rested, pushed again. The stony surface did not give, of course, not even the tiniest fraction of an inch.

After a while I sank to the stone step and huddled there. People would look for me. Of course they would. How long would it take them to find me down here? Days? Weeks?

And then I realized that no one might open that trap door for years, because only Lisa and Kevin knew of its existence, and Lisa would never tell, and Kevin, probably, was in New York now, or halfway to Europe.

I felt a rawness in my throat, and knew that I had screamed. Some part of my mind that was trying to hold me together said, "You mustn't scream. If you start screaming, you'll go mad."

It was the blackness, the utter blackness, that made me think of insanity. If I could have some sort of light, even for only a few moments, perhaps I could think, despite this pain in my head. Perhaps I could even find a way out. For instance, there must be some sort of air pipes, probably in the tunnel. If I had a light, maybe I could find them. And when this terrible storm was over, I could scream through them, and maybe someone up there on the blessed, blessed earth finally would hear me.

The lantern. Perhaps Lisa had left the lantern with which she had struck me down. Perhaps she had left the matches, too.

Now only dimly aware of the pounding pain in my head, I groped my way down the stairs, up the sloping tunnel, and into the cavern's hollow roar. My heart leapt as my hand, moving over the table's surface, encountered the lantern's metal base. Swiftly, eagerly, using both hands, I felt all over the table top. No matches. I dropped to my hands and knees and felt all around the table. Nothing but sand and pebbles.

Crawling, I began to move over the cavern floor, stopping every second or two to search around me with my hands. I was whimpering now, and I could feel tears flowing down my face, and although I knew it was dangerous to whimper like that, just as it was dangerous to scream, I couldn't help it.

My head struck something, and for a few seconds I saw points of colored light in the blackness. Where was I? Had I crawled in a circle back to the table beside the tunnel's entrance? I reached out and felt rough woolen cloth. A blanket. I must have struck my head against the foot of the bed.

And near the foot of the bed, I remembered now, was that steel door, shutting off the small natural opening in the outer cave's rear wall. I felt a sudden wild hope. Perhaps the waves, hurtling up the beach to pound against that area of weakened limestone, had enlarged the opening. If I could swing the door back . . .

Standing up, I reached out a hand and found the cavern's rough wall. I moved my hand a little to the right. It found the steel door, the hasp, the bolt.

I withdrew the bolt. Something struck my shoulder —the door's steel edge? a wave-borne rock?—and sea water roared through, a foaming, ghostly phosphorescence in the blackness. I staggered backward, lost my footing, and went down into several inches of water. I lay there for a moment to gather my ebbing strength, and then tried to stand up, but another wave smashed through and sent me staggering back against the table.

Get that steel door closed! I waited until another wave had cascaded through, and then waded as rapidly as I could across the cavern. My groping hands found the steel door and tried to swing it across the opening, but sand and pebbles must have lodged in the space between the door's edge and the limestone wall, because it swung only a little way. Knowing that by now the sea had gathered itself for another assault, I turned. A wave foamed through, almost sweeping me from my feet, but I managed to reach the table.

I clung to its edge. "No use," I thought. My head throbbed unbearably, and already there was salt water in my lungs. I could not shut the sea out, and I could no more get through that opening, and through those turbulent waves, than I could get through the trap door.

How long would the waves smash through that ever-enlarging gap in the wall? For many, many hours, certainly. Even after the wind died, those high seas would keep rolling in. And the water, already well above my knees, would keep rising here in the cavern.

No use to tell myself now that I should have waited to open that steel door, waited even for days, if necessary, until I could no longer hear the waves' roar. I had not been able to think clearly, and so I had opened the door. And now I could not think of anything to do except go back to the stairs, and crawl up them, and huddle there under the trap door.

And if the water, rushing down the tunnel's slope, rose higher and higher in the shaft until it reached the top? Well, it would not matter, because even before the water touched me, I would have become quite mad.

Already the madness was starting. Through the roar of water, I thought I could hear Harley's voice, calling my name.

I heard it again, and turned around. Was he really out there—somewhere beyond that opening in the cavern wall? A faint hope stirring, I moved forward. Another wave smashed in, almost knocking me from my feet, but I struggled on through water that swirled around my thighs.

"Jennifer!"

The sound was closer now. Screaming an answer, I lunged forward, thrust a hand through the opening, felt it clasped. Another wave rushed in, drenching my face, but I pushed my other hand through the foaming water. Harley's hand closed around it. With no sense of pain, I felt myself dragged through the jagged opening, felt arms carrying me.

Another wave caught us as we emerged onto the beach, and I felt Harley stagger, but he held onto me and turned toward the limestone steps cut into the bluff. Dimly I was aware of the vast and raging sea out there, and wind that tore at us, and the stinging salt water in my lungs. A second wave struck us, but we were on higher ground now. Then Harley shouted in my ear, "I'm going to put you on the steps! Crawl!"

Limestone edges under my hands, across my shins. I crawled upward through blinding rain. At the top of the bluff I staggered to my feet. Then Harley was there, lifting me, carrying me along the broad path between the wind-tormented trees. We were past the branching path that led to the pavilion now. Soon I would be in the house.

But no. He had struck off on a path that angled toward the cottage. Vaguely I wondered why, but it did not matter. Now that I had been delivered from that nightmare world below ground, nothing else mattered.

He carried me up steps, through the lamplit kitchen, into the bedroom where another lamp burned between the two framed photographs on the bureau. He set me on my feet. Hands on my shoulders, he asked, "Are you hurt?"

His face, I saw, was gray with exhaustion beneath its tan. I said, from a throat that felt raw from the salt water I had swallowed, "My head—"

"Let me see." I bent my head, and he gently parted my hair. "The skin isn't broken, but there's a big lump. We'll get to a doctor tomorrow to see if you have concussion." He turned, took the gray flannel robe, and handed it to me. "Go into the bathroom and strip off those wet clothes."

I obeyed. In the bathroom I knotted the robe around me and then, too exhausted to pick up my wet clothing, left it on the linoleum. The wind, I suddenly realized, was dying now, although rain still drummed on the roof.

I went into the bedroom. He stood beside the bed, a glass holding about an inch of amber liquid in his hand. As I moved toward him, he turned back the blanket. "Get in."

I lay down, and he covered me with the blanket and handed me the glass. "Get it down as fast as you can."

I gulped the bourbon. Then, with its warmth spreading inside me, I handed him the glass. He placed it on the bureau. Sitting down in the straight chair beside the bed, he rested his head in his hands.

It took me several seconds to realize that it was more than exhaustion which made his wide shoulders slump. I said, "Harley?"

He raised his head and looked at me. "Lisa's dead." His voice sounded dull. "She'd almost made it back to the house, but a falling tree caught her . . ."

He told me then how, during the hour-long lull in the storm, he had rowed a rubber raft from the power boat used in the rescue work to the dock at the island's northern end. "Right after I got into the house, the wind started up again. I went upstairs. You weren't there, and neither was Lisa. I went out to look for you."

He'd found Lisa pinned under the trunk of a slash pine a few yards beyond the entrance to the beach path. "I had a flashlight. Later I lost it down on the beach, but I had it then. I could see that her eyes were open, and she was alive. I got down on the ground, so she could hear me, and asked her if she was in pain. She said no."

He had known, with despair, what that meant. Her spinal cord was smashed. So as not to lessen any faint chance she might have, he had not even tried to lift the tree.

"She said to me, 'I'm going to die.' I told her that was nonsense, but she said, 'Yes, I am, Harley.' And then she said, 'Jennifer's in the cave. I think I killed her. I had to do it. I'm sorry.' "

He said, grief and dull wonder in his voice, "She looked and sounded so damned young. I can remember when she was still a nice little kid, eight or nine, say, she'd sound like that when she apologized for losing my ball-point pen, or for taking a page out of one of my college notebooks to draw pictures on."

He had tried to question her. "But she just muttered nonsense. Then her eyes glazed over, and I couldn't find her pulse, and I knew she was gone."

Because he hadn't known of any other cave, he had gone down to the one on the beach. Between waves, when most of the water had flooded out, he could see that I wasn't there. "I was sure you had been swept out to sea. Then a big wave rolled in, the one that tore the flashlight out of my hand, and I saw water pouring through that opening, and realized there must be a cave beyond."

He stopped speaking. After a moment I said, "She did it because I found out." He looked at me with those bleak eyes, and I went on reluctantly, "I found out that she'd killed Aunt Evelyn."

214

He nodded. "I was afraid she had. All along I've been afraid of it."

Neither of us spoke for a while. In the silence, I could hear that the rain had dwindled to a gentle patter.

Finally he said, "Your mother must be very worried."

I sat up. "You woke her?"

"Yes, and Amy Warren, too. I had to ask them where you and Lisa were."

I swung my feet out of bed. "I'd better go to her."

"All right. We'll go up to the house."

Twenty-Four

As I have said, Dolor Island is now in the hands of an estate agent. Its actual sale, of course, cannot be completed until the probate court makes its decision. Despite the affidavits my mother and I filed concerning that holograph will, and despite Harley's affidavit renouncing any share in the estate, the probate court is still making up its ponderous legal mind.

But as my mother says, it's all academic anyway. Since the island is to be sold, what difference does it make whether she or her son-in-law holds title in the meantime?

She is being a bit premature when she refers to her son-in-law. Harley and I will not be married until the middle of December, after he finishes his commercial pilot's training course at a school a major airline maintains in Arizona.

In one of his recent letters he said, "The desert is beautiful, especially at night. When I stepped outside a few minutes ago, I felt I could almost reach up and touch the stars. But I could never live inland. Sometimes I miss the smell and sight and sound of the sea almost as much as I miss you.

"I'd like for us to live on an island someday. Not Dolor Island, of course, but some island, someplace."

My first thought was, "Never!" To me an island would always mean Kevin, with his engaging grin and his spurious war wound. Corrupt and ultimately unlucky Kevin who, carrying almost a pound of heroin from that metal box in the cavern, got as far as St. Augustine airport that morning—only to be stopped by a Federal marshal, armed with a description furnished by the man with the scar. An island, too, would always mean Lisa, staring down at that bit of blue-and-white cloth in my hand.

And then I thought of other things about the island. The tang of salt air and the fragrance of pine, with the rich odor of subtropical earth underneath. I thought of blue water stretching away from a white, blessedly empty beach, and of pelicans grotesque and yet graceful against the sky, and of Harley's outstretched hand with a shell lying on its palm. Most of all, of course, I thought of Harley himself, whose natural element seemed sunlight and the sea.

And so I wrote back, "All right, darling. Maybe an island. Some other island, someday."